WITCH BONES

J. Cortex

Other stories from J. Cortex:

Carnivores

Other stories from Lantern House:

Sugar Skin
Trial 23
Carnivores
Blackwood Manor

Lantern House Publishing

This is a work of fiction. Names, characters, places, events, and incidents are either products of the author's imagination or are used fictitiously.

This book is the intellectual property of Mr. J. Cortex.

Published by Lantern House Publishing, Nanaimo, B.C

https://www.lanternhousepublishing.com

Edited by Nicholas Wilson.

ISBN: 978-1-9991734-1-8

WITCH

BONES

CHAPTER ONE

1

Dawn's light shined through Talbert and Lani Schmidt's bedroom window with the same golden brilliance it did every morning since the completion of their country home, ten years prior in the late spring. Talbert yawned and opened his eyes. The sun was warm against his face and he basked in it a moment, let his eyes drift shut and kept them closed a second longer, then looked to his wife, Lani, who lay comfortably next to him in a nest of pillows.

Talbert smiled and kissed the back of Lani's head. "God bless our souls," he said, "for the Lord has seen it fit to make me the happiest farmer on two legs, and you my bride."

Talbert swung his feet out from under the white duvet Lani had spun together the previous winter using a bundle of sheep's wool she had traded over in Fort Boise for a sac of good quality corn. "God's light shine on them boys over at The Hudson Bay Company," she had told Talbert. "Good lot, they are."

Talbert stood and stretched his weary bones. He walked around the bed, to the window, and looked out at the bright new day. It was spectacular. Talbert had built their bedroom on the east side of the house on purpose, so the sun would wake him in the mornings, and so he could enjoy the stunning view of the countryside without leaving his room. Talbert loved waking to the sight of rolling green hills and blue skies, the sound of birds chirping and the sight of their aerial bodies darting in and out of the trees. It reminded Talbert of how generous God had always been to him. It reassured the middle-age man that moving west had not been in vain.

As he stood with his arms folded over his hairy chest and his eyes scanning the beautiful countryside, Talbert thought back on the ugly disorder he had once risen to as a boy in Cincinnati.

2

Tired and sore, Talbert woke each day as a child to the sound of whining horses and the ring of the blacksmith's hammer. The youngster grumbled and pawed sleep from him eyes, then rose from his thin mattress and crept across the cramped attic, having to hunch to keep from bumping his head on the low ceiling, to the window. Only, it was not a window so much as a hole in the red brick skeleton of Schmidt & Son's General Goods, the business his father owned.

From the fracture in the wall, Talbert had a bird's eye view of Main Street. He used to it to observe the city with the curiosity of a young boy.

Talbert watched the hustlers shamble down the block in beaver hats and trim suits through an early morning twilight. He saw women in flashy dress, all puffy and frilly and fancy, and wondered where they were going. Talbert also saw grungy cowboys canter through the smoke that rolled out of the blacksmith's shop and filled the street like a fog, riding horses that Talbert thought majestic and battered from war. He liked those men, with their larger than life hats and the spurs on their black boots, their pistols always reflective no matter how much filth covered them.

The folk Talbert did not like were the disheveled drunks stumbling or being shoved out of Bernie's Saloon across the street. Their hats were always tattered and their trousers always soiled, their beards untrimmed and wild. Sometimes they sat in front of the building and spewed or reached into a hidden pocket of their coat and retrieved a flask. Sometimes they fell asleep and Talbert had the pleasure of watching a deputy come by and give them a swift kick in the gut with his freshly shined boot. Talbert liked the deputies. The guns of order, the fist against the scum. He liked the way people treated them, how someone would nod and shake the hand of whichever deputy they passed on the street, all smiles and, "God bless ye."

    Talbert's father, Eli, also despised the sin-seekers who ruled Cincinnati. He was a God-fearing man, one who attended church every Sunday with his family. Him and his wife, Molly-May, ushered their litter of three down the clogged streets to the church, every one of them speckled in their neatest attire for the occasion. They sat front row and gave selflessly when the collection plate came around. Sometimes, Father Maxwell invited the Schmidt family over for dinner on Sunday evenings. That was how exalted Eli Schmidt was in the community.

    Yes, Eli Schmidt was a God-fearing and law-abiding man. He built his business from scratch at a young age, married Molly-May before they had ever lay together as man and woman, and thanked the Lord for every meal. These traits were passed on to his children, and Talbert became a devoted Catholic at a young age.

    Talbert was educated at Sister Cleo's Catholic School with the other boys of his pedigree. He was tight of lip and sharp of mind, and never had an issue with scholastics or behavior. He learned the sales trade from his pa, and woke bright and early seven days a week to watch Main Street come alive. He peered down at the strangers and wondered where they were off to, and why they all appeared so angry, then crept across the attic abode he and his sisters shared and woke the girls. After breakfast, Talbert walked to school, and after, helped his father in the store until closing. It was during those hours that he observed how Eli interacted with his customers, both the pleasant and the unruly sort, and discovered a great deal about people.

"You need to listen to people," his father told told him one evening after work, sitting in the back of the shop on some wooden crates while Eli smoked a cigarette. "You don't know if the lady who's just walked in is a widow, if her husband died ten minutes before. You don't know if the dirty fellow with coal smeared over his face is the richest man in the east, or if the bloke in fancy cloth is a beggar. You simply *can not* know someone by looking at them, Talbert, and you need the patience and earnest want to find out. What you discover will shock you at times. I promise you that, son. At other times, it may repulse you. Sometimes the things people divulge to you will make you want to cry, or laugh, or any manner of thing. But what you need to remember, Talbert, is that God fit us each with a different soul, and all in his image. Remember to respect everyone as if they were your brother, and always have the courage to open your heart to them."

Talbert did remember. If there was one speech his father ever gave in all his life that stuck with him, it was the one from the night in the dimly lit storage room of Schmidt & Son's General Goods.

3

Standing now in the house he had built with his own sweat and blood, Talbert ran his hands along the smooth wood of the windowsill and recalled the sanded surface of his father's shelves, stacked to the brim with odds and ends, trinkets and doo-dads. It made him smile.

Talbert decided to let Lani sleep another twenty minutes and went into the kitchen to prepare some java, and perhaps reminisce just a little more.

Talbert could see his crops from the kitchen window. He lit a match and set the coal stove to warming, then gazed out at the long rectangle of soil that was bordered by a low fence. There were rows of potato plants there, perhaps four-hundred spuds in all. Behind them were long stocks of corn. Talbert had planted the seeds at the beginning of the season, and soon would come harvest, which happened to be his favorite time of the year. Him and his son, eight-year-old Johnathon, would head into the field at sunrise with beige sacks and pull the gritty vegetables from the ground until they were sore and filthy. Lani would come later to assist with the corn. The day always ended as a family affair and all-around good fun.

To the left of the field was the chicken coup. It was a small red building that housed two dozen chickens. A short wooden ramp led to the closed door and it smelled, as Jonathon put it, "Like when the outhouse is too hot in the summer and you have to plug your nose while you do your business. Gross!"

The outhouse, in fact, was behind the chicken coup. Talbert thought it was a good idea to keep all the foul smells in one area. No one disagreed with him on that.

Talbert's tool shed was on the other side of the crops. It was not quite as glamorous or as cute as the little red chicken coup, but it did its job, and that was fine with him. Beyond the shed was the pasture. It went on for miles, rolling green fields to the horizon and to the south of them the forest.

The stove top was hot from flame and Talbert placed a metal canister on it, then looked back out the window. Daisy and Fiona meandered lazily through the meadow a few yards away. Jonathon had named the cows at five-years-old, even though Talbert had already named them Becky and Bruce, since one was a male and the other was female. But with Jonathon's decree they were renamed, and both became girls. Where the boy had come up with the names, Talbert and Lani were clueless.

Taking his eyes out of focus for a moment, Talbert caught sight of his reflection in the glass and decided he needed to shave after morning chores. His stubble was growing a tad too stubbly for his liking.

Talbert yawned and walked over to the kitchen table. He took a seat and waited for the water to boil, again thinking back to his father's shop.

It had taken Eli half his life to establish a respectable business in Cincinnati. His father had come from England as a boy and had brought with him money. That helped. Determination helped more, and by the time Talbert was born things were booming.

However, Eli did not much care for Cincinnati itself. He loathed the saloons and the brothels, the boozers and the mine men. He did not care for the noise or garbage that never seemed to leave the sidewalks. But he loved his business, and on the day that Talbert made the firm decision not to spend his adult life in that cesspool of trash, and voiced as much, his father had calmly said,

"I know this town stinks, my boy. I know. It's full of sinners and instigators. But there are decent folk here, too. God-fearing folk. Besides, we make too good a living to try elsewhere and in time, God will cleanse the tragedy of this place."

"But that man stabbed the other man in his neck," a young Talbert said. "He just stabbed him, pa. He called him names and killed him, right there in front of all the people and no one did a darn thing."

"Watch your mouth," Eli said. "And listen close. I'll not let a bully leech me of my spirit or scare me from my home. God in Heaven will see to that scoundrel, and be our shield against his ilk. As for moving, forget the idea. I've poured my life into my business and when I'm gone it will be yours. The house I built will be yours. Everything I do now I do for you, and of course for God. When you have a breed of your own, Talbert, they will dictate your actions as you dictate mine now. It may seem strange to you at this moment, but in time you will come to understand. As a man, I hope you have the strength not to let your life be ruled by fear of devils."

Talbert nodded, confessed that he understood, and agreed to discard any notion of leaving Cincinnati. It was the first time he lied to his father. As an adult, Talbert still felt shame for it.

The water bubbled inside its cage. Talbert rose from his reverie and filled the upper chamber of the drip coffee pot with black dust, then poured the boiling water over the grounds. As he waited for the coffee to filter, leaning against the counter and looking dully across the kitchen, Talbert's memories turned grim.

Eli Schmidt died of a whooping cough during one particularly harsh winter when Talbert was eighteen. It had come on fast and ended faster. Talbert was seated at the dinner table with his parents when the first attack occurred. Eli lurched, his plate of potatoes and corn and fresh baker's bread soaring from his hands and spilling onto the table, and began to hack.

It was gentle, for a second. He wheezed a bit and shards of potato were spat from his mouth. But it persisted. Eli strained, breathless, and his face flushed until it was as dark as a beat. His veins bulged from neck to forehead and he pounded his fists against the table and fumbled for purchase. And he coughed. He coughed and coughed and fought for breath. He sucked in air whenever he could and spittle flew and drool oozed and Molly-May and Talbert looked on in horror.

What Talbert still remembered, as he stood daydreaming in his kitchen, was how scared his father had looked. Never had Talbert witnessed his great and powerful pa afraid of anything, ever. Yet as Eli struggled to simply breathe, his eyes popping from his skull and darting wildly about as if he could find something to save him...

Well, that was a striking image.

So striking it had haunted Talbert all through his life, and when Eli passed away six weeks later in a cold hospital bed with blood in his uncut beard and his eyes fogged over, twenty pounds lighter, the image of his pa gagging at the dinner table was still more terrifying than the sight of an emaciated Eli, frozen stiff under a bland hospital sheet.

A grown man standing in his kitchen, Talbert shivered.

His thoughts then drifted to two years later, when his life in Cincinnati had come to a devastating end.

After Eli passed to the other side, Molly-May—though she knew he was in God's kingdom—became depressed. "To fill my time," she told Talbert, "and my heart, I am going to stay in the new hospital on the west side of town and give my time to the Sisters of Christ's Faith."

Talbert smiled and told her it was a wonderful idea.

"My children are grown," she said, "You are busy with the store and with the pretty girl I see you courting. Your sisters are nurturing children of their own. With your father gone, I need a place to put my energy and faith. I know Eli would have supported me on this."

Talbert had been happy for her. She went away and sometimes she came for dinner in the apartment above Schmidt & Son's General Goods and informed her son that everything was going just great, that she was helping so many strong, Catholic souls.

Unfortunately, like all the other sisters at the hospital, Molly-May was exposed to the brave trailblazers who rode into town vomiting and shitting their trousers, bursting with cholera, typhoid fever, tuberculosis, and other ravages of settlers. Also like the other sisters at the hospital, it did not take long until Molly-May contracted an unknown ailment, and fell hopelessly ill.

The house doctor had her figured for TB, but her

condition progressed so rapidly that he was unsure. She was admitted to the same ward in which she had caught the cursed disease in the first place, and suffered a long, drawn out, and painful death.

Talbert and his sisters had taken turns sitting by their mother's bed. One of them was always by her side, every night until God claimed her. At the time, Talbert was pursuing Lani's hand in marriage, and as the situation with Molly-May worsened, he recruited his future wife to help at the store and sometimes accompany him to the hospital for a long and miserable night of watching Molly-May writhe in agony and cough up blood.

Her misery lasted six months.

Molly-May had been lethargic through it all, and occasionally delusional. She lost control of her bladder and shed pounds at an alarming rate, often crying the whole night through. In the end, her death was a blessing. Talbert never did say it out-loud. He only thought it. Yet even by thinking it Talbert felt shame. But it had been hell. Pure hell for everyone. His sisters were both caring for tiny infants and the stress of having to make the trip to the hospital every other day was too much for them to handle. As for Talbert, he had a store to run and a woman to flatter. Besides the obvious emotional distress caused by watching his mother waste away to a corpse, something barely human—and it was a lot—he had a life of his own to live, and they all knew Molly-May was not coming back. "She is in God's hands," they all said.

And God let her slip through his fingers.

4

Remembering those dreary nights brought a solitary tear to Talbert's eye, and he quickly wiped it away.

The coffee was done. Steam rose from the press and into Talbert's noise. He retrieved two porcelain mugs from the cupboard and filled each to the brim with hot black sludge, then took a sip and peered out the window. Daisy had wandered from Fiona and was grazing off in the distance. The sun had climbed too high, Talbert knew. His morning had been eaten by reflection.

He tried to pull his mind out of the dark pit it had fallen into by making a list of chores for little Johnathon to do when he woke up.

Sweep the floors.
Clean out the chicken coup and feed the chickens.
Fetch water from the well.
My father's bloodshot and bulging eyes.
No.
Milk Daisy.
Churn a new batch of butter.
My mother's taut, ghoulish face when I peeled the sheet away to look in her glassy eyes.

"Stop," Talbert said, shutting his eyes and pinching the bridge of his nose. "Stop this foolishness. You're not a boy anymore. You can't dwell on such things."

It was hard not to. Once the box of memory had opened in Talbert's mind it was difficult to close. Images of his mother and father in their worst states of decay tumbled out, unfiltered, to cycle through his head and reopen old wounds. He felt like a boy again, sitting with his head cradled in his hands and struggling to overcome a nightmarish daydream.

"Talbert?"

Lani stood in the doorway, wearing her white nightgown. Talbert had not been crying, but it felt like his eyes were puffy and probably red. "Oh, good morning, Lani."

"Good morning," she said, "and a blessed morning at that. Is everything quite alright, dear?"

Talbert sighed. "Yes, everything's fine. I was just thinking."

As Lani walked into the kitchen, she regarded Talbert with the same inquisitive hazel eyes he had fallen in love with as a teenager. They always saw straight into his soul. "Thinking about what, dear?"

"The past. My father. My mother. A whole shipload of memories spilled loose this morning. I haven't even woken Johnathon yet."

Lani smiled. She sat down beside Talbert and picked up her steaming coffee, took a sip. She slid her hand over his, her skin warm against Talbert's cold knuckles. "It's been a while since you've talked about them. Why today?"

Talbert thought. He looked around the room, frowning, then his gaze fell on Lani and he grinned. "Well, I just haven't the slightest notion, to be honest."

"No matter," Lani said. "Sometimes it's good to remember, even if the memories hurt."

"Yes. I think so too. Besides, the unfortunate passing of my father—having to watch him suffer like that, followed by the six months of my mother's anguish, led us west. It was God's plan after all, and maybe this morning he needed to remind me of the sacrifices it took to get us here."

Lani smiled. She released Talbert's hand and cradled her coffee. "That could very well be the case, dear. Sometimes we need a reminder from God, so we don't forget why, or how, we got to where we are, and who got us there."

"You should have been the preacher's wife," Talbert said, teasing.

"Now, now, Talbert. You don't need to be a preacher's wife to speak the wisdom of The Lord. You know that."

"Aye, so I do. No woman preaches it better than my wife."

She smiled and so did he. Lani looked beautiful and five years younger that morning, as she always did with a bit of sleep in her eyes and her brown curls wild. Talbert, shirtless and hairy, a tad too stubbly, looked very much his age.

They sipped their coffees and after a while Talbert said, "Do you like our life here, Lani? That is, do you like our life here better than what our life would have been in Cincinnati?"

She raised a dark eyebrow. "Are you having doubts? Has sifting through old memories uncovered a naughty little seed of doubt? You know how devilish doubt can be, dear."

"Not doubt." Shaking his head and looking into his mug. "Something else. Curiosity, I suppose. I'm thinking about the trip here, after I sold the shop to Mr. Hannah and we packed up and left, not knowing where God would lead us."

"To prosperity..."

"Or straight off a cliff."

They both looked glum into their mugs, smiling thinly. The jest was half funny, half a serious reminder of the immense risk they had taken by leaving Cincinnati. Now that it had been mentioned, Lani and Talbert could not help but pause and think back to when they first embarked on the journey west with nothing more than two good mules to pull their wagon and all their belongings tied down between its rickety wheels.

The ugliness of their situation had been that neither of the newlyweds had the slightest clue as to where in the great big blue world they would settle down. Sure, Talbert and Lani had heard of settlements on the coast, towns that had sprung up across the mid-west and to the south. On the other hand, they had also heard of the reputations of these growing cities, full of thieves and outlaws. Lani and Talbert wished to find a more peaceful commune, quiet and without violence, a place where the Lord's light shone brightly.

They also needed to survive the arduous trip to their new home. Food and water were not big issues, for wild game and clean rivers were in abundance. The danger came from the cruel diseases that ravaged travelers and left many new world seekers dry bones in the dust of the prairies. Not to mention the bands of criminals, savage marauders, rapists and lunatics that claimed sanctuary in the unpopulated mountains and expansive forests of the new land. Lastly, there were the Indians to contend with. The red men who burned wagon camps to ash and feasted on the pale occupants, or so Talbert and Lani had been told.

"I still can't believe we made it," Talbert said. "The hazards we avoided. The hardships we overcame. The things we saw. It was a true miracle our wagon ever rolled into Emmert."

"By God's grace, so it was," Lani said. "Never had I dreamed of discovering a hub of safety in such godless chaos. And I couldn't in all my life of asked for a warmer welcome. The folk here were the real miracle. They were the real gift from God."

Talbert gave a nod. "Aye, when I saw the tall wooden gate and how it's pillars were shaved into thick spikes--" Talbert gestured with his hands the tall pillars of Emmert's defensive wall. "Well, I dare say I thought we had stumbled upon a fortress of scalp-hunters. But when Sheriff Rackem came to greet us—when those wooden gates swung open and the snow sprinkled street appeared, the humble cabins glowing with lamplight, the gentle folk looking curiously on at us—Oh, how disheveled we must have appeared! And Sheriff Rackem ushered us inside. Well, it felt like I had just been welcomed home. Dare I say, it just felt right."

"Yes, dear. I feel the same."

"For Rackem to have offered us this plot of land—well, that was almost too generous. It was lucky we had the money from my father's store to afford the wood to build this house, and things like this new coal stove." Talbert pointed to the giant cast iron stove near the window, the black chimney a long cylinder ascending through the roof.

"And Fort Boise is only a four-day ride. The lads over at The Hudson Bay Company had just about everything we needed to create this paradise. Anything they didn't, well they sure found. Heck," Talbert said, grinning, "do you remember the day I came home with that set of glassware, the ones with flowers etched into the sides? You looked about to faint."

"I was sure surprised," Lani said. She stood and collected their empty mugs, placed them on the counter. "I'm not sure how I feel about Fort Boise, though." She wrinkled her nose. "Bit of a slum."

"Aye, it's no place for families. The men in Fort Boise are rugged forest men. I reckon they drink and gamble, and I've got my suspicions about the company of women they keep. But the traders are fair and decent, and for that alone, I pray to God to bless them, and help direct them away from sin."

Lani smiled and nodded. She looked out the window at the bright green day. "It's getting late. Noon is just around the corner."

Talbert sighed. "Aye, so it is. I suppose I should dress and wake Johnathon."

"Yes, and I'll make everyone an egg and slice up some of that bread Miss. Huntly brought over yesterday."

"Sounds great, dear." Talbert stood and gave himself a tired shake. The grim memories of his departed parents were already fleeting. "That woman bakes the softest, most delicious bread on this side of the pond. It was awful nice of Miss. Huntly to bring us a fresh loaf."

Lani agreed. She pulled three eggs and the loaf of bread from the small pantry while Talbert shuffled towards their bedroom. He felt ready to face the day.

5

Talbert slipped his feet into a pair of warm, woolly socks that reached his knees and pulled on his favorite black boots, the ones with the silver spurs that clicked when he walked. They were Sheriff Rackem's old pair. He had given them to Talbert as a gift.

Talbert and Sheriff Rackem had become quite close in the twelve years since Talbert and Lani entered Emmert's gates on that cold winter morning, frosty and unbathed and looking more than a little deranged. Rackem had taken them into his home, which doubled as the town jail—never used—and the sheriff's office. He sat them down in front of the roaring hearth and went to fetch a bottle of cheap whiskey. Of course, Lani and Talbert refused the toxic stuff on account of being good, wholesome Catholics, and so Rackem made coffee while the couple relaxed and let the warmth of his fireplace dissolve the bitter cold that had seeped into their bones, a dreadful condition they thought never to be rid of.

Sheriff Rackem returned with two steaming mugs of coffee and his guests nodded their thanks. He sat in his reclining chair and poured himself a glass of warm, yellowish whiskey, then leaned back, stretched out his legs and rested his boots on the brick mantle of the fireplace. Rackem grumbled to himself as he rolled a cigarette, then bent and struck a match on the leather of his boot. He cradled the wavering flame and squinted as his cigarette erupted, as the paper flared and a surge of smoke rushed past his face. Then he flicked the match into the fire.

"Right, let's get to it," Rackem said. His voice was rough, eroded by gallons of whiskey and as bristled as his face. "First off, I need to know where you've come from. We can move on after that."

Talbert glanced at Lani. They were both bundled heavily in deer hides and their faces looked small, pale. "Cincinnati," Talbert said.

Rackem considered while he drew on his smoke. "Cincinnati..." The word rolled slowly off his tongue, like it was foreign: *Siiin-sinnn-atti.*

"That's right," Talbert said. "We've been roaming northwest now for... Well, I dare say I don't know how long. Perhaps a year. Maybe two. Only God can say for certain how many days we've spent rambling along wagon trails, up mountains and back down again, through plains of dust, forests without end..." Talbert trailed off and stared dead-eyed into the flames, haunted by the memories of those desolate places.

Rackem grumbled and blew smoke through his nostrils. "As is so often the case. God tends to count the things we can not."

"Aye," Talbert said, "so he does."

Lani raised a dark eyebrow. "Are you a man of God, Sheriff?"

"I reckon we are all men of God, Ma'am. I'm inclined to assume your curiosities lay more in the realm of whether or not I am a *godly* man. Whereas, do I pray to the Lord of Creation, or do I spend my days in sin, in the company of whores and villains."

Lani's silence said he was correct in his assumption.

Rackem grumbled. His expression was hidden beneath the shadow of his hat and all Lani could see was the black bush on his jaw shifting as he spoke. "I suppose it's only natural. For if you say true and Cincinnati was indeed the home you fled—in search of greener pastures, no doubt—then I know well the road you traveled. Savage beasts roam it, as you're surely aware, things lesser than men. Witches, too. They lurk within these western woods, though you'd be hard pressed to come upon one and tell the tale. Few are."

Now it was Rackem's turn to stare dully into the crackling hearth, as if he too had been besieged by sudden memories.

"Nevertheless," he said, "after such a long march down that road of lost lives and abandoned hopes, sickness and strife and monsters of the kind, and as winter's frigid winds beat down upon you and the world is a white, frosty purgatory no less, an end appears through the snow. Yet instead of coming face to face with a more desirable character—a ginger fellow with spectacles and a lovely wife, perhaps—you're sat down before me, a worn-out old sheriff."

Lani thought a smirk parted the thickness of Rackem's beard, though could not have been sure.

"A man," Rackem went on, "who as I'm sure you've noticed is unmarried at the gray age of thirty-nine. A man who dresses like a sinister gunslinger. I appear a dark denizen of Hell itself in this black jacket of mine, I know, and my hard-to-love face obscured below the brim of my wide hat like the Reaper himself. An unlikely friend, to be sure. I also know that the stench of whiskey and stale smoke permeates throughout my home, similar to any whorehouse one might stumble into across this new nation. No Ma'am, not a whiff of ladies' perfume to be found in my den, nor the elegance brought by a wife's gentle nature. My house is disorganized and cluttered, uncouth in its arrangements and lazy in its upkeep. My fault, without doubt."

The sheriff tilted his head back and inhaled loudly, spat a wave of white smoke at the ceiling.

"But I yammer. My apologies. Let me answer your inquiry so I can put your minds at ease as best I can. You see, I understand your skepticism of me and my secluded town. But let me assure you Ma'am, though I may be a rare and ugly sight, I would not harm a hair on any decent man's head, be they red, white, or any variation otherwise. And let me be clear that here in Emmert, we do not harbor fugitives, criminals, thieves, murderers, rapists, practitioners of evil--"

Rackem spewed the list of rejects from his mouth like scraps of sour tobacco.

"Or any of their ilk. This is a place for peace and prosperity. We have zero tolerance for violence or ill-will of any kind. I can proudly say that as sheriff, I have never once had to commit someone to the crude jail I've built in the cellar of my house, nor have I needed to act as lawman because of some overconfident drunk or disgruntled husband. There is simply no hatred here. The people of Emmert are as kind and docile as a herd of grazing doe."

Rackem took a sip from his glass and grimaced at the strength of it, the burn of the poison. Then he pinched his fleeting cigarette between stained teeth and inhaled, flicked it into the fire.

"Still," he said, smoke curling out of his mouth, "I am their protector. You could call me the wolf that protects the sheep. It's a title I flaunt with great seriousness. This town is a bright example in a world of growing darkness, and I won't see it marred by allowing one bad egg to breach these walls and hatch. That's why I ensure that only the purest of pilgrims enter here."

Talbert and Lani nodded that they understood, though Rackem's attention was fixed on his boots, black as grease in the firelight, and they doubted he saw them.

Rackem said, "We produce quite a generous harvest in the fall. Almost every family who lives here began as unsettled vagabonds, just like yourselves, stumbled upon this place by accident. I sit everyone down, just like this, and we either strike a deal or we don't. If we come to an agreement, the new citizens of Emmert are welcome to a plot of fertile land and encouraged to build and to merge with the community. Those I turn away are sent off with nothing, pointed in the direction of Fort Boise."

Rackem shifted in his chair and placed his feet on the floor. He tilted his hat upwards and, for the first time, looked Talbert in the face, then Lani. The couple were shocked at how Rackem's icy blue eyes radiated out of his dark, weary visage.

"The reason I'm telling you all this is because you've entered my home humble in your frost-crusted furs and I believe you to be good-natured and deserving of a chance, especially after your hardship. What I'm saying is, I would like to offer you a place here. We have good land come spring, and a warm hearth for you to rest beside until winter's cruel grip on the land fades."

Talbert and Lani did not know what to say. They peered at each other in utter shock, in disbelief of everything Rackem had just said. Four hours ago they had been lost in the snow and so hungry that their remaining mule would have been dinner by nightfall. Now they were offered land and friends and a secure home. It was a lot to take in.

Rackem tilted his hat down and a shadow encompassed half his face. He started to roll another cigarette. "You don't have to answer now. Drink your coffee. Think. Talk amongst yourselves. As for my relationship with God, or my godliness, as you were so interested in." He paused to strike another match and light his smoke. "Let me just say that God's wrath is as real to me as it is to you, and that no man fears it more."

6

Talbert rolled the sleeves of his linen shirt up to his elbows, just the way he liked them when toiling in the field on a hot day alongside his only son. He enjoyed the heat on his forearms. It reminded him of something he could never quite place. He buckled his belt and put on his big straw hat, then went to wake Jonathon.

Talbert's farmhouse was not large. From his and Lani's room it was a short trip down the hallway to little Jonathon's door. The scent of fried eggs and fresh bread followed Talbert the whole way.

He knocked on the boy's door. "Rise and shine, Johnathon. You've had the whole morning to sleep. I think you know God's view on laziness."

There was no reply from within.

Talbert twisted the knob and pushed open the door. There was no one inside.

Johnathon's bed was empty. The blankets were tousled as though he had risen in the night to pee but never returned. The small dresser Talbert had built for him was undisturbed and the oil lamp on its surface was unused. The window was closed. The curtains were drawn.

"Johnathon?" Talbert stepped into the room, more than a little confused. He looked under Johnathon's bed. Nothing there but dust and a carved horse head on a stick. He stood up, glanced around. There was no place for Johnathon to hide.

Talbert fled to the kitchen. "Lani," he said, short of breath, "have you seen Johnathon?"

She shook her head. "No, of course not. He's in bed, is he not?"

Talbert's eyes were wild. "His bed is empty, Lani. Can you see him outside?" Talbert did not wait for an answer. He raced out the back door and onto the porch, where he stood with his hand to his brow, scanning the yard.

Lani came out behind him, flustered with her arms folded tightly across her chest. "What do you mean he's not in his bed?"

Talbert ignored her. "I don't see him out here. Check the house, quickly. Look out front. I'll look in the chicken coup." Talbert dashed down the stairs and into the yard, shouting Johnathon's name. But Johnathon was not in the chicken coup, nor was he hiding in the tool shed. Talbert found no trace of the boy inside the corn field or out in the pasture. Lani found no sign of him in the house.

Lani and Talbert Schmidt searched their property all morning. They never found Johnathon.

CHAPTER TWO

1

Sheriff Rackem woke in a pool of sweat. The cotton sheet of his bed was soaked and his whole body was moist from it. He felt like a slug. Even before he groaned and opened his eyes, Rackem knew he was going to be sick. He rolled over and puked a yellow slop onto the floor.

Then he lay there gawking at it, the ooze spreading over the old floorboards. Rackem had not eaten the night before. No wonder he was vomiting whiskey and stomach acid. It made him embarrassed, angry with himself. He was a useless drunk and he knew it. He rolled onto his back and shut his eyes, pulled his fur blanket to his nose and tried to get warm. Despite the daylight breaking in through the cracked panels of his home, Rackem shivered.

He spent the next hour in misery, laying in bed with the shame of last night at the forefront of his mind while he waited for the queasiness in his belly to subside. Rackem kept mumbling to God for release. He prayed that God would forgive him.

After a while, Rackem's sickness settled and he sat on the edge of his bed in his ratty underclothes. He stared dumbly at the black fireplace in the corner of the room and its rusted flume. He did this for a long time, remembering all those years ago when he had installed the outdated thing. It felt like a lifetime ago. He supposed it was.

Rackem fetched his pouch of tobacco from the bedside table and rolled a cigarette with trembling hands.

Scraps of brown leaf sprinkled his blanket. He sparked a match and lay back and smoked, blew noxious fumes at the ceiling. It was dark up there, much like his conscience. Rackem could see where a spider had made its home between two joists, its web silver and flimsy.

He snuffed out the cigarette on his bedside table. His glass from last night still had a finger of whiskey at its bottom. There were a few flies in it. Rackem groaned, hating himself as he poured the rank stuff down his throat. It was rancid and made him gag, like drinking kerosene, but it kicked his ass out of bed. Rackem got up and picked a dead fly from his teeth. Then he got dizzy and fell against the wall. Not even noon and Rackem could barely walk. He braced himself against the wall of his bedroom, the whole miserable world spinning.

"Come on, useless old fool. Get moving."

He shuffled across the room with his hands before him like a blind man. His clothes were dumped in a pile by the fireplace. A mound of black rags, boots and jacket and rider's pants. Everything was filthy, stained with dirt from Rackem digging in the woods last night. He really had looked like a graverobber out there beneath the trees, hunkered in the moonlight as he clawed at the dirt.

Rackem picked up his clothes and went to wash the filth off them.

2

Sheriff Rackem's house was not the luxurious homestead of Talbert and Lani Schmidt. It was not that new. Rackem had built his cottage twenty odd years ago. Back then there was no Emmert. There had been only fertile land, untouched by man. Rackem had built Emmert brick by brick. He had given the town its name and handpicked every resident and given them plots to farm. He was Emmert's father, really. Its father and its caretaker.

The sheriff's office had come much later, after the town had swelled in size. Rackem had built it in conjunction to his little cabin, which was quite modest compared to the other residents' homes, like that of Talbert and Lani. Rackem's cottage was but a room with a stove and a table, a bed, one window, cast iron pots and pans hung from hooks and a few lanterns dangling from the trusses. Rackem had used one of the lanterns last night when he snuck off into the woods to dig up his box.

Leaving his apartment, Rackem carried his clothes into the sheriff's station. It was four times the size of his room. Even the foyer, where all the doors in the house connected, was larger than Rackem's private chamber. There was a writing desk hectic with papers, a cabinet in the corner with rows of stained whiskey bottles. The only time Rackem ever used the space, which he thought of as his office, was to sit at the writing desk and pour himself a glass of whiskey; and on occasion write a birth certificate or perform the other duties of a town sheriff.

Then there were the doors. One to Rackem's chamber. One that led to the parlor where Talbert and Lani Schmidt had sat on their first day in Emmert. Another led to the front porch, and another to the backyard. The final door, an odious thing made of scorched timber, descended to the cellar. Rackem had built it as a holding cell, yet the only thing the cellar ever held was Rackem and his demented thoughts. The lonely sheriff spent too much time drunk and muttering to himself in the dankness of his basement.

The yard was overgrown. Weeds crawled up the fence and the patch of soil where Rackem had once tried to grow tomatoes was home to a family of critters. Even the outhouse was falling apart. The wood was cracked and warped and needed new paint. Rackem figured he would need to rebuild it soon.

The old sheriff went straight for the well and the washing drums. He dumped his armload of dirty clothes into one of the drums, muttering, "Fool," as he hoisted up a pail of water from the well. Then Rackem washed his clothes with a bristle brush until the water was brown and his clothes were dreary black, just the way he liked them. He hung the garments on a line and gave himself a brisk wash. Then he went back in the house, away from the bright light. It was making his head throb.

Rackem poured himself a glass of whiskey while he waited for his clothes to dry. He needed a bit of drink to stop his quivering, to make himself feel normal. Besides, Rackem had nothing to do. Not really. The sheriff's involvement in the town had been dwindling recently. He had been drinking more and more, cowering deeper within himself. He was more of a hermit now than a town sheriff. Peeling back the curtain, Rackem peeped cautiously at the outside world.

Across the street, Mrs. Ashberry was sweeping dust off her front porch. She smiled and waved at Mr. Beucanon as he led his mule cart towards the wooden gates of Emmert, his cart piled high with beige sacs and wooden crates from his wheat mill. He was bound for Fort Boise, more like than not. Young Thomas Weathers opened the gate for Mr. Beucanon and waited until him and his mules were outside before closing it. Then Thomas went back to leaning against the redwood pillars and chewing on a stock of grass.

Rackem sighed and let the curtain fall back in place. Thomas was more of a sheriff than Rackem was, the young boy standing guard by the gate day and night. Hell, even fat Mrs. Ashberry was outside more than Rackem these days, always out there sweeping her porch and waving at people. It made him ashamed. So ashamed that Rackem poured himself another glass of whiskey and went into his room to stare at the box he had dug up.

What a cruel thing, the dirty strongbox set against the wall underneath the faded portrait of his mother. It was made of thick rosewood and reinforced with steel. It had brass fixtures and a big brass latch, a heavy lock dangling from it. Only a madman could pry the thing apart—maybe Logan, the blacksmith. But Rackem had a key. He had taken it from beneath a squeaky floorboard last night to open the box. A mistake, no doubt. But what was done was done. All Rackem could do now was stand in the depressing silence of his room and stare at the cursed thing, wondering what in the name of God had coaxed him into digging it up and opening it.

Twenty some years since Rackem had buried that box. One night of whiskey and a deranged ghost screaming in his head to open it.

3

Lani stood on the porch and watched Talbert ride off their property. She would remain home in case Johnathon wandered in the front door. Poor boy, lost out in there world without his mother. She had no idea where he could have gone. His window was shut, curtain drawn. Johnathon had simply vanished.

Talbert kicked his horse down the Emmert Road, gusts of wind pushing his brown hair about. He reached the Roscal's farm in under a minute. They only lived next door, their properties separated by a thick hedge of trees. Talbert tied his horse to the Roscal's fence and went up to their house.

Pete Roscal was lounging on his porch in a big wicker chair, drinking a glass of lemonade when Talbert Schmidt unlatched the gate and strolled across the lawn. Pete smiled and waved. "Talbert, what in the world brings you to my farm on such a blessed and sunny day? Are you here to bring us some eggs?"

Talbert tried to give Pete a neighborly smile. Talbert's lips spread and quivered and he looked sadder than anything. Talbert was afraid that when he spoke, his voice would crack and he would let spill an ocean of tears. For the love of God, Talbert's boy was missing!

"Good morning, Pete," Talbert said. "Sorry to dissappoint you, but it's not eggs that bring me here this morning. It's my boy."

Pete's smile faded. He put down his glass of lemonade and walked to the edge of the stairs. "What's happened to your boy, Talbert? He sick?"

"Nah, I don't reckon." Talbert put his foot on the bottom step and paused. He was not sure if he had the strength to lift the other leg. His body felt like clay.

"What is it then?" Pete asked.

Emily emerged from the house and came to stand beside her husband. She wore a plain green dress and was at least a head taller than Pete, who was unusually short and almost totally bald. "What a nice surprise," she said. "What are you doing here, Talbert? Have you come with eggs?"

"He hasn't come with any eggs," Pete said, frowning. His tone slapped the smile off Emily's face.

"Oh. What is it then? Is everything alright?"

"Actually, it's not." Talbert sighed, pinched the bridge of his nose and looked up at them. "You see, I went to wake Johnathon this morning, like I always do for morning chores. But he wasn't there. He isn't anywhere. We checked the house, the field, the stables. Everywhere. We just can't find him."

Emily gasped and covered her mouth. Pete's frown deepened. "Dear God," Pete said. "Where do you wager he's gone?"

Talbert laughed the saddest laugh Pete and Emily had ever heard. "I don't know. Johnathon's only eight. He doesn't go off wandering. He's never left the farm without Lani or me. I can't for a second imagine him running away. It makes no gosh darn sense."

"You must be devastated," Emily said. "If our precious Angela ever went missing, I think I'd collapse upon the ground and never rise."

"Aye," Talbert said, "dare I say Lani's not far from that herself, if she's not bundled up in a corner already."

"I'm sure he could not have gone far," Pete said. "You'll find him. No doubt about it."

"I pray you're right," Talbert said. "The reason I came by is to ask if you've seen him. Obviously, you haven't."

Emily looked more upset than Talbert. "No," she said, wringing her hands, "I'm sorry. I wish we had."

Talbert sighed. "Me too."

"We'll go out into the fields right away and have a look," Pete said. "We can poke around our property, see if your lad got lost and wound up sleeping under the deck or curled below the apple trees."

"Thank you," Talbert said. "I'll go up the road and ask the Tanner's if they've seen him. After, I'll go to the Oswalds, then the Henleys. Someone ought to have seen my boy."

"God willing," Emily said.

Talbert was about to leave, had half turned around when he stopped and looked back. "One other thing. Have you seen any strangers on the road? Anyone at all?"

Pete and Emily exchanged a baffled glance and shook their heads. "No," Emily said. "I haven't heard a horse since the sheriff's went by last night."

4

Someone was knocking on the door. It woke Rackem from his weird daze. He had been staring at that damned box for an hour. "Who is it?" he called from his chamber. Rackem's clothes were still on the line. He was dressed in his tattered, sweat-stained underclothes.

"Me."

"Oh, hell." Rackem grumbled to himself. "What is she doing here?" He recognized Miss. Huntly's perky voice. She was the only one in Emmert who sounded so chipper all the time, constantly elated. Rackem put his glass on the table by his bed and went to open the door.

A petite creature with blonde curls and sparkling blue eyes beamed at the disheveled sheriff. Larissa Huntly stood on the porch in a flamboyant pink summer dress, crowned with a matching bonnet. She radiated love and warmth and all kinds of fuzziness. Rackem always wondered how Larissa could be so happy since she was alone, her husband rotting in the dirt.

"Good afternoon, sheriff." So much zeal Rackem flinched. "I have been knocking for hours. I thought perhaps you were still asleep." She gave him a narrow look. "You weren't, were you, still asleep?"

Rackem cleared his throat, trying not to breathe on Larissa. His breath reeked like whiskey. "No, of course not. I was hanging clothes up to dry. I didn't hear you knock."

"That's my sheriff, always working."

Rackem gave her a thin smile, a little crack in his black nest of a beard. "What can I do for you, Miss. Huntly?"

Larissa was so excited. She had to huff in a lung of air before she said, "Well, sheriff, it's not what you can do for me, but what I can do for you. I know you're a busy man with town business, and I know you hate people coming over to bother you unannounced, but I thought I should come by and share some of the Lord's cheer." She pulled a loaf of bread from behind her back and presented it to him. "Fresh from the oven, just for you, sheriff. Well, not fully fresh. I baked it last night. But the hour was late and I didn't want to disturb you. I know how you hate to be disturbed. I could never bother you like that."

So many words. Larissa made Rackem's head spin. She was tiny and enthusiastic with her toothy smile and frilly perfume made Rackem's nose twitch. He grunted and gestured for Larissa to come inside.

Larissa Huntly was a thirty-year-old widow with extraordinary good looks and a figure that rivaled the youngest, most desirable dame in any big city. She was the most beautiful woman in Emmert by a mile, and had been married to Yohan Huntly, a wealthy settler from Scandinavia. When Yohan died five years past, due to an accident involving a cheap bottle of moonshine and a sickle, his unfortunate widow had been left bored and lonely.

But Larissa liked Emmert. Even though there were no single men in the town for her to claim, she refused to leave. Rackem had a hunch she was sleeping with people's husbands.

Rackem put Larissa's bread on his writing desk and sat in his chair, Larissa standing in the doorway with her hands folded at her waist. She said, "Pardon my manners, sheriff, but may I say something?"

"You may."

"It stinks in here. I mean it, sheriff. It smells like a saloon, like smoke and stale booze. I say, your house smells like a tavern." She looked around, at the clutter and at the dirty state of the place. "And it's filthy. Just filthy."

Rackem made a face. "Suppose the floors could use a scrub. Though I've hardly the time to crawl on my knees scrubbing the floorboards. I'm too old for all that."

Larissa got a feverish gleam in her eye, smiling slyly at Rackem. "That is exactly why you need a wife, someone to help you out around the house."

Oh no. Not this again. Miss. Huntly had been hounding Rackem for years about finding a wife. She wanted to take him to Fort Boise, or even on a trip to the big city, to find a suitable woman. Really, Larissa was just bored.

She was saying, "The good Lord made us in pairs, you know. It ain't right to be alone, sheriff. It just ain't. You'll perish here by your lonesome, all them liquor bottles as company."

Rackem glanced past her, at the shelf of bottles. Everyone knew he was a drinker. No one said anything about it. Rackem's affair with whiskey was his own business. The townspeople quietly accepted it.

"I'm too old and too tired for a wife," he told Miss. Huntly. Rackem wanted her to leave. He hated sitting there in his gross cotton breeches looking like a used-up old fart. "I really do appreciate the bread. Hand to God, I do. But if there's nothing else, Miss. Huntly, I should really get about my day."

Larissa looked like she wanted to say more, her mind spinning for an excuse to stay. Her eyes were all over the sheriff's disorganized mess of a home, fingers twitching as though eager to strip off her fancy pink dress and pick up a broom. "Are you sure there's nothing you need help with, sheriff?"

Rackem pushed his chair back and stood up. "Quite sure." And reached past Larissa to open the door. "God bless you, Miss. Huntly. You and your bread are welcome any time. I really must get to work now."

Reluctantly, her face pinched in frustration, Larissa curtseyed to Rackem and stepped onto his porch. "Blessed day to you, sheriff. We will talk about this wife business later."

"Can't wait."

Rackem watched Larissa walk down his stairs and into the dusty road. She waved to Mrs. Ashberry, still sweeping her porch like a lunatic. Then Larissa sauntered up the lane looking absolutely lost, a lonely widow with no where to go and no one to talk to, nothing to do but tend to her house and bake bread. Rackem felt sorry for her. He should have invited Miss Huntly into the parlor for some coffee or a lemonade.

Just then, Talbert came thundering down the Emmert Road on his horse. He blew past Miss. Huntly and went straight for the sheriff's house, Rackem still standing on the porch in his breeches. Talbert tied off to Rackem's broken fence and hurried to greet him.

"Talbert," Rackem said, "you look pale."

Talbert could not contain himself. He blurted, "I fear

the worst. I can't keep myself composed any longer, Rackem. It feels as though the Lord's light has ceased to shine and the world is cold. By God, Rackem, I'm cold!"

"Talbert, calm down. What's happened?"

Talbert paced, Rackem standing in his doorway confused. "He wasn't at the Roscal's, not at the Tanner's, and certainly not at the Oswald's. One disappointment after the next. No one's seen him. Not a darn soul. He's gone, Rackem. He's gone and my heart's fit to burst."

Rackem did not understand. "Who, Talbert? Who's gone?"

Talbert stopped pacing, looked at Rackem with wild eyes. "My boy, I tell you. My boy's gone, snatched from his bed in the night."

Rackem's heart lurched. "Impossible..." Then he saw the crowd in the street. Young Thomas Weathers, Miss Huntly, Logan Reitner—all standing in the dust, watching Talbert and his hysterics. Even Mrs. Ashberry had stopped sweeping to gawk.

Rackem took Talbert by the shoulder. "Come inside. Tell me everything."

5

They went quickly into the parlor, where Talbert collapsed into a chair. He sniffed and wiped snot from his nose, telling Rackem, "I woke, same as I do every day. I went into the kitchen and made coffee. Lani came out. We talked of days past. It was nice. Everything was okay." Talbert paused, a horrible sensation washing over him. His jaw started to quiver. "Then I went to wake Johnathon. I just wanted to wake my boy. Only, he wasn't in his bed. He wasn't outside. He wasn't anywhere."

Rackem scrunched his face as he lit a cigarette, bare feet propped on the mantle of the fireplace. "Tell me more. Tell me about Johnathon's room."

"There's not much to tell. His bed was messy. It looked like he had gotten up in the night to relieve himself, then never returned. The window was closed. There was no sign of an intruder. I went to look in the yard and he wasn't there. He wasn't in the chicken coup. He wasn't in the stable. I don't know where he could have gone. He just vanished. I'm losing it, Rackem. I'm terrified."

Rackem could see Talbert's terror plain as day; he could feel it. Twelve years they had been friends. Rackem had never seen Talbert in such disorder. "Does Johnathon have a hideout?" Rackem asked. "A secret place in the woods? Lots of youngsters like to play out there."

Talbert shook his head. "No, he's only eight. He's never even been in the woods. I can't imagine him fleeing there in the night. It's not like Johnathon at all."

"It could be that Johnathon had a bad dream," Rackem said, funneling smoke from his hairy nostrils. "Had a bad dream and wandered off confused, got lost some place. It's not unheard of."

"Or it could be that he was taken," Talbert said. "What if someone took him? What if someone came into my house and stole Johnathon while Lani and I slept, then snuck off with our boy?"

Rackem shook his head. "There are no kidnappers here. Not in Emmert. No one in this town would have taken your boy, Talbert. You know that as well as I do."

"What about the Injuns?" Talbert looked serious, even mad. "What if the Injuns are upon Emmert? What if they've taken Johnathon to cook him and eat him? Those godless savages. They could come back tonight for someone else's child. God's love, Rackem, what if the Injuns attack the town?"

"Calm down, Talbert. You're acting crazy." Rackem shifted in his seat, wondering if a band of rogue Indians really had made it to Emmert, were camped in the woods near Talbert's farm. It was a worrisome thought. It was not something Talbert needed to have rattling around in his head. "There are no Indians for miles in any direction," Rackem told him. "You know that."

Talbert sighed, utterly destitute. "I don't know what to do." He hung his head. "Johnathon didn't run off. He'd never do that to us. Something's happened, Rackem. I can feel it. A hollow has opened in my soul. It feels like my light has died. Johnathon's my only son. Where in God's name is my boy?"

Rackem had no answer. He was at a loss. None of what Talbert said made any sense. Boys did not simply vanish in Emmert. Not in Rackem's town. Even if there were Indian's around, they did not typically steal children. Wild Indians were butchers. If it had been Indians, Talbert and Lani would have been hacked to pieces and Lani raped.

On the other side of it, Rackem knew Talbert's boy. Johnathon Schmidt was a happy, energetic child, full of life, eager to help his ma and pa around the farm. Rackem could not see the innocent kid shifting away in the night. Not on his own.

Yet who could have taken him?

Rackem flicked his cigarette into the fire and stood up. "We'll find your boy, Talbert. I promise."

And that was when purpose flowed into the alcoholic sheriff for the first time in years. He scowled at the dead fireplace, feeling strong with duty, with resolve. He had to find Talbert's boy. He had to find out what had happened.

"Best go home, Talbert," Rackem said. The call to duty had him standing with his shoulders broad and his eyes deathly serious. "Go home to Lani and pray to God that we find your boy before nightfall. I'll gather the townsfolk for an emergency search party. We'll comb every inch of this town until will find him."

6

It appeared an Invasion.

Mid-afternoon and the Schmidt family farm was besieged by an army of farmers and women in simple dress, their children running circles around the horses that feasted on Talbert's well-kept grass. They numbered close to fifty, and Sheriff Rackem was their leader, seated on his ebony mare in his black duster and wide brim hat. He was not even drunk.

Rackem nudged his horse through the crowd to the steps of the Schmidt homestead, where Talbert and Lani stood on the porch in each other's arms, looking fearful for their child. Both were tormented by Johnathon's absence. Talbert felt like the worst father in the new world. Lani was in shambles, her face wrought with distress. Talbert held her close and petted her head.

"We need to get moving," Rackem said to them. "The sooner the better. This light won't last forever."

Talbert gave him a nod. He whispered in Lani's ear, "I will find our boy," and kissed her on the cheek. Then Talbert walked down the steps and joined the bulk of Emmert, those warm townsfolk kind enough to help search for his son.

Rackem dismounted and approached Talbert. "I have a special job for you. Mr. Beucanon left a few hours ago with a wagon and some mules bound for Fort Boise. I want you to catch up with him and relay your troubles."

"Why?" Talbert asked.

Rackem lowered his voice, so not to be heard by the others. "I was thinking about what you said, about someone stealing your boy. If it is true, they might turn up in Fort Boise. If you can get word to Martin Beucanon and have him pass the message along to the boys at the fort, and they see a stranger wander into town with a youngster matching Johnathon's description, they'll lock him up on sight. It's worth a shot, Talbert. Better to explore every avenue in this type of situation."

"What a great idea," Talbert said. "Wow, I knew there was a reason God saw it fit to make you sheriff. You're a clever man, Rackem."

"Go now," Rackem said. He did not need compliments. "Ride hard and catch Mr. Beucanon before the night comes."

Talbert thanked the sheriff and went for his horse. Rackem corralled the folk of Emmert and sent them to their tasks.

Men with hounds were sent into the forest behind Talbert's house, while the women and children were ordered to sift through the fields surrounding the Schmidt home. Men on horseback rode off to inspect the nine farmsteads between Emmert's core and the Schmidt's front porch, while even more men on horseback rode out to the northern road. It was a well coordinated search, and Rackem had high hopes they would find Johnathon within the hour. He gave Lani, still lingering on the porch, looking pale and thin in her nightshirt, a nod of his hat. Then Sheriff Rackem guided a regiment of farmers down the Emmert Road, where they became obscure in a haze of dust.

7

It was dark when the first search party returned. Lani was waiting on the porch. She had stood there for hours, watching the sun slowly sink in the western sky and melt through a crop of trees, witnessing the death of light and the rise of a darkness that strangled the world. There had been voices to hear earlier, the name of her son, distant, carried to her on the wind. But that had died out long ago.

What Lani heard now was the thumping of a great many feet from around the house. She broke the crescent moon's spell and raced down the steps, a frail ghost in her night gown. She turned at the bottom and ran to the corner of the house, pivoted and nearly crashed into Mrs. Ashberry, who let out a squeal.

"Lani! What in God's name are you doing? You frightened me half to death."

The plump Mrs. Ashberry clutched her chest, a signal that her heart had indeed nearly exploded from fright. Who could blame her? Lani was so eager to see her son that she looked insane. Her eyes were huge and black. Her teeth chattered. Her hair was tangled and her gown was translucent in the stark gloom. It was no doubt Mrs. Ashberry mistook Lani for a crazed phantom gliding through the darkness.

"Well?" Lani said. "Where's Johnathon? Is he with you?" She looked around Mrs. Ashberry, scanning the long formation of exhausted women and kids. They had been combing the countryside for hours. "Johnathon? Johnathon?"

He was not there, and Mrs. Ashberry and the other women looked ashamed of it. Many averted their eyes in humility. They felt guilty because they would return home with their children while Lani cried herself to sleep.

It was Mrs. Ashberry who met Lani's desperate gaze. "He's not with us. I'm sorry, my dear, I am. You know I lost a girl at your age. Twelve years old when she got sick. Her name was Beth. She was the sweetest child, bless her soul."

Lani wanted none of it. She staggered away from the fat bitch with her stories of tragedy and her promises of understanding, back onto her porch. Lani sulked in shadows until the women had gone.

Riders came a little later. They rode one by one through the Schmidt's open gate and dismounted their horses. Pete Roscal was the first of the dusty men to cross the lawn and reach the bottom of the porch, where Lani stood gazing up at the moon. The others clustered in behind him: Logan Reitner, Daryl Mason, Stanley Weathers.

Pete took off his hat and held it against his breast. "Mrs. Schmidt, the men and I searched until past dark. We went to every farm between here and Emmert, mine included, and combed the nearby country. We even poked around in the mill. There was no sign of your boy."

Lani said nothing. She was an ethereal statuette and her gaze was fixed on moon.

Logan Reitner stepped forward and he too removed his cowboy hat and pressed it to his heart. "Perhaps on the morrow, Ma'am, I could offer my services to look for your boy. I can be ready at dawn."

Lani did not answer Logan. She was frigid in her pose and seemed unmovable. The loss of her boy had crippled her, turned her mute and insensible.

Pete put his hand on Logan's shoulder and said, "I reckon you ought to talk to Talbert in the morning. Mrs. Schmidt is in no state."

Logan nodded and placed his hat back on his ruffled black hair. He said to Lani, "God be with you, and with your family," and started for his horse.

Daryl and Stanley followed Logan, but Pete lingered. When his comrades were out of earshot, he glared up at Lani with cruelty in his eyes. Pete said to her, "I'm glad your fucking boy is gone. He's getting fucked in Hell." Then Pete left, dawned his hat and walked to his horse.

8

The men who had searched the southern forest returned soon after to find Lani in a vegetative state. They relayed the same unfortunate news and after being denied a word of thanks, or any word at all from the silent mother, sauntered off and were swallowed by the blackness at the edge of Talbert and Lani's farm.

Thirty minutes later, a shady figure in a wide brim hat materialized out of the gloom and rode slow and deliberate to the house.

It was Sheriff Rackem. He nudged his horse up to the house and disembarked. He stood at the foot of the stairs and rested one hand on the butt of his flintlock pistol. The light of the moon gave Rackem's gaunt face the illusion of being that of a corpse, pallid and decayed.

"There was no sign of Johnathon on the road," he said to Lani. "We pushed hard to the north. To the south, too. We rode out to where the land becomes hostile and flat and the desert begins. We saw nothing. I assume by your silence the others didn't find him either."

"Heaven," Lani murmured.

Rackem grumbled. "Let's not go there. Not yet. We don't know that your boy is gone to the Lord's house."

The sound of an incoming horse made Rackem turn his head. He watched the road as the thud of hooves grew closer.

Talbert galloped out of the dusk and into his yard. He left his horse beside Rackem's ebony steed and hurried over to the sheriff. "What's the news?"

Rackem cleared his throat. How did you tell a man his son had been stolen? "No luck, I'm afraid. Everyone gave it their best. We searched until the sun went down, but the darkness made it impossible to hunt any longer. It doesn't look like Johnathon's anywhere near here. I'll need to start an investigation tomorrow."

"An investigation?"

"That's right. It may be like you said. Someone may have taken your son."

Talbert buried his face in his hands. "It's as I feared," he moaned. "Some godless beast has stolen my son while I slept, and in my own house. God forgive me."

"No," Lani said, still gawking up at the moon. "My son lives in God's house now."

Talbert gaped at her. "What did you say?"

"God's taken him home. Johnathon is up there, in Heaven." She pointed to the glowing moon. "There is no need to worry."

Talbert was outraged. "Don't you dare! Johnathon may be gone, lost in the wilderness or taken by a stranger, but he lives. He's alive and I'll find him, God be praised. Don't say such things."

"No." Lani was clearly disturbed. "Not stolen. Not lost. God came. Or was it an angel? Whoever it was reached into Johnathon's bed and lifted him up, ascended to Heaven with our boy." Lani smiled as she spoke. The content smile of a crazy person.

Talbert looked at Rackem. "What's she talking about?"

Rackem didn't know. He shrugged. He and Talbert stared at Lani from the bottom of the porch, her hand outstretched as if to cradle the moon in her palm.

CHAPTER THREE

1

Talbert Schmidt barely slept. For the longest hours of the night he lay in bed and stared at the ceiling. Restless, Talbert suffered the voice in his head, the one whispering from his conscience, telling him to go out in the forest and search for his son, to be a father and find his boy.

And there was another voice, one telling Talbert his son was dead and all hope was lost, and that God had forsaken him.

He got up once, went into the kitchen and looked out the window. The meadow was murky in moonlight. Going out there would be foolish. Talbert knew as much. What could he find in the night that a dozen men had missed in the day? Nothing. Talbert would only stumble blind through the timbers and get lost.

But he felt so hopeless! So helpless! His son was out there somewhere, either lost in the woods or kidnapped—and Talbert could do nothing. And Lani, his beloved wife, was still on the front porch, muttering praises to the moon.

Talbert went back into his room and eventually fell asleep. His mind could only withstand so much abuse, so much torment before it collapsed. His body rested, and his mind slipped into a disturbing nightmare.

2

He was the air itself, a shapeless entity flying across the forest, through gnarled branches and sleeping ravens. The forest was gloomy. An eerie fog rolled over the ground.

The vapory mist parted beneath Talbert and he saw Johnathon, his dear son wandering through the dusky thicket. The child was afraid, glancing nervously between the timbers. He scurried to the husk of a redwood tree and climbed into its cavity, pulled his knees to his chest and waited, blinked out at the shifting twilight mist as it closed in around him. All Talbert could see were his boy's white, blinking eyes.

Then something came walking.

From outside the boundary of Talbert's vision encroached a thing he could not see, yet could feel. The grove darkened at its presence and grew cold. The ground rumbled. The birds stirred and squawked and fluttered off into the night.

Whatever it was, Johnathon could see it. His eyes grew wide in terror and he clawed up and out of the hollow, then dashed deeper into the misty forest, trying to get away.

Talbert was an unhinged leaf. He fell and was carried along the wind behind Johnathon—drifting, spiraling, topsy-turvy, his view of the world dizzy and unfocused and Johnathon's upside-down legs scrambling over stumps and struggling through barricades of entwined branches.

Talbert landed on the forest floor in front of Jonathon. He saw the fear in his son's face and it made Talbert want to scream. Johnathon's mouth was wide, huffing air as he dashed through trees, fleeing from the monster. It came into Talbert's view, a gargantuan beast lumbering through the grove. It was gangly and its head broke through the canopy, snapping branches as it strode forth on ungainly legs and swung arms too thin for its body, this emaciated giant with rotted, gray skin.

Johnathon fell, tripped over a root and did a face plant in the dirt. He rolled onto his back and cried out, scuttled backwards on his elbows. The great goblin of the forest exploded through the fog and reached its mutant limbs for the boy.

3

"Johnathon!"

Talbert sat upright in bed, soaked in sweat. It had just been a dream. A horrible dream. He tried to hold onto the image of his frightened son, but the nightmare was already fleeting. Talbert had already forgotten the grotesque giant. The details of his flight through the midnight forest sank into the dark recess where dreams go to die.

Lani was still not in bed. Talbert wasn't surprised. His wife was disturbed, all night blabbering about Heaven and trying to touch the moon. He rolled out of bed and went to go find her.

But she wasn't on the porch where Talbert had left her. He stood in the doorway, curious how he had slept for so long. The sun was at the top of the sky. It was close to noon. Talbert must have been truly exhausted to have slept so late. He frowned at all the hoof prints in his yard and went back inside.

On his way through the house, Talbert stopped to check inside Johnathon's room. It was still clean, toys piled in the corner. He had hoped to find Johnathon sleeping beneath his blanket or playing with the box of dominos Talbert had traded in Fort Boise last year. But there was no Johnathon. No Johnathon and no Lani.

He found her in the back. Talbert entered the kitchen and immediately spotted Lani through the window. She was in the yard, looking like a wax phantom, some romantic ghost standing guard over her lover's tomb—if her lover's tomb was the farm's well.

Talbert went outside and crossed the grass and came upon her, Lani staring expressionless into the depth of the well. The reservoir was a circular stack of bricks with a wooden crank above, the bucket dangling on its rope. "What are you doing?"

Lani said nothing. Her brown hair was a mess, the position she was bent in rather holy, as if Lani was at prayer. She looked like an angel of the morning in the afternoon's bright light.

"Have you not slept?" Talbert asked. "Will you take no rest?"

He took Lani's hand in his, her flesh cold and her fingers limp. Talbert tucked her hair behind her ear and kissed Lani's cheek. "Wake up, my love. Come back to me."

She just stared into the hollow of the well, unblinking.

Talbert looked. There was nothing, darkness and a thicker darkness below. He said, "Johnathon?" And Talbert's voice echoed back at him. There was no way Johnathon had fallen in the well.

"Hell," Lani said, her voice a timid squeak.

Talbert seized her by the wrists. "What did you say?"

"Hell."

"What do you mean Hell? Who's in Hell, Lani?"

Her face was dull, empty. She chanted, "Hell. Hell. Hell. Hell."

"You've gone mad," Talbert shouted. "In the name of Jesus Christ and all that is holy, you've gone mad!"

"Hell. Hell. Hell. Hell." Flat. Ritualistic.

Talbert was dumbfounded. "You're possessed," he said. "You've lost your wits. I can't take it anymore. Stay here and chant until your tongue falls out, Lani. I'm going to find our son. With or without you."

Lani pointed a bony finger at the well. "Hell. Hell. Hell. Hell."

4

Early afternoon the day after Johnathon's vanishing and Rackem did not have a single whiskey in him.

He was leaned over the railing of his porch with a cigarette in his teeth, out in the sunlight and not drinking alone in his cellar. It felt good to be alert for once. Nice not to stink like alcohol. Nicer still not to have a headache. Rackem's hands still trembled—he figured they always would without whiskey. But at least he was clear of mind. Rackem had a job to do. The Schmidt boy was missing and Rackem needed to him.

Mrs. Ashberry was still sweeping dust from her porch, and Rackem watched her suspiciously. How much dust could there possibly be? He wondered if she was going mad like Lani. Rackem could not forget how deranged Talbert's wife had acted last night, groping for the moon, rambling about angels. Grief, he knew, was a killer.

Other than the fat old lady and her broom, the only person outside was young Thomas, slumped against the gate while he gnawed on a blade of grass. It was so quiet. Rackem thought he had lost a day somewhere. It felt like Sunday, all the citizens of Emmert tucked inside Pastor Marble's church, the crazy old man. Pastor Marble was older than Jesus himself. He woke from the dead to give a mind-numbing sermon every Sunday, then hibernated in his church the rest of the week.

No, it could not be Sunday. Perhaps the whole town had slept in. Even Rackem, for being dead sober, had slept past dawn.

Rackem spat his cigarette into the dirt. It was time to get started. He walked to the stairs, put his hands on his hips and looked around, not a damn clue where to begin his investigation. If Johnathon was not lost somewhere around Emmert, which he wasn't. Fifty people had searched ten square miles and not found a trace of the boy. Then someone had taken him. One of Rackem's trusted citizens had Talbert Schmidt's boy tied-up in their house, in their stable, in their cellar. Rackem needed to find out who. And if it mattered, why.

This meant asking a lot of questions to a lot of people. Mrs. Ashberry seemed like a good start. She was right there on the other side of the street, one of Emmert's oldest residents neurotically sweeping her porch. Rackem tread down his steps and across the road, his spurs jingling as he went.

"Morning, Mrs. Ashberry."

Mrs. Ashberry stopped sweeping and looked down at him. She seemed confused, like Rackem had broken her from a trance. "What a surprise, sheriff. A bountiful morning to you, too."

"Is it alright if I come up and speak with you?"

She leaned her broom against the railing and folded her arms over her bosom. "Course, sheriff. Come on up."

"I know you're a busy woman these days," Rackem said as he thumped up her stairs. "I wouldn't want to interrupt your chores. I certainly don't want to bother Walter. How's he doing, by the way? I haven't seen him out in a while."

"Walter's just fine," Mrs. Ashberry said. "He's sleeping now. He sleeps most of the day. Ever since the accident, Walter doesn't go out much, as I'm sure you know, sheriff."

"Yes, so I do." Rackem had been there when Walter Ashberry was crushed by a felled tree last summer. Its huge trunk had broken Walter's legs, confining him to one of Logan Reitner's wheeled chairs for the rest of his life. Mrs. Ashberry was the caretaker to her crippled husband.

"I see Miss Huntly is a frequent visitor of yours," Mrs. Ashberry said, cheeks plump and rosy in a grin. "When are you going to propose?"

Rackem guffawed, a guttural snort. "No, no, you've got the wrong idea."

"Shame," she said. "The girl's pretty."

Rackem straightened his hat, feeling embarrassed. "I'm here to ask if you've seen anything strange recently. Someone out of place. Maybe someone acting unusual."

"Oh dear." She put her hand to her breast. "Is this about the Schmidt boy?"

"Afraid so."

Mrs. Ashberry puffed out her cheeks, fluttered her eyelids. "Geeze, sheriff. I haven't seen a thing out of the ordinary in the eighteen years Walter and I have lived here. Yesterday's manhunt was the most exciting thing to ever happen in Emmert."

"Yes," Rackem said, "it was the first day I had to act as sheriff in any serious capacity. A sad day for Emmert."

"A sad day for Lani Schmidt," Mrs. Ashberry said. "The woman was in tatters last night when I saw her, just destroyed. Poor woman. Even the town is upset, sheriff. The streets are empty. The air is tense. Not even the birds are singing."

Rackem tilted his ear and listened. Nothing. No tweets. No caws. No sound at all. It was too eerie for such a nice day.

"Will that be all?" Mrs. Ashberry asked. She seemed flustered, anxious for the sheriff to leave.

Rackem made a face. He did not want to pry, but he felt like he had to. "I'd like to talk with Walter."

"No," she said. Mrs. Ashberry crossed her arms and shuffled in front of the door, as if Rackem would try to fight his way inside. "Walter's asleep and I won't wake him. Not even for you, sheriff. My husband needs his rest."

Rackem gave Mrs. Ashberry a weird look. He had known her and Walter nearly two decades. Rackem was used to Mrs. Ashberry's peculiarities. But this was strange, even for her. "Alright," he said, "fair is fair. I won't bother Walter."

Anyway, Rackem was hardly concerned about Mrs. Ashberry's enormous rump getting in and out of Talbert's house unnoticed. And Walter. Well, he couldn't even walk. "I'll get out of your hair," he said. "I have a lot more doors to knock on before my day is done."

Mrs. Ashberry grinned, fat cheeks bulging like a toad. "Thanks for stopping by, sheriff. God be with you on your search."

Rackem started down the steps, rolling a cigarette as he went. Something about Mrs. Ashberry bothered him. He thought she really was going mad, guarding her house like a hound. Maybe Rackem would check in with her later.

5

The street was deserted. The sound of Rackem inhaling tobacco was loud without any wind or the banging of Logan Reitner's hammer. Logan's blacksmith shop was closed. So was the general store. The homes all appeared vacant, like the population of Emmert had slunk away in the night. On the corner was Miss Huntly's quaint little cottage. No one looked to be home.

Thomas Weathers was the only one around. The kid squatted against the main gate and watched Rackem stroll over to him. Who better to question than the gatekeeper? Thomas was outside every day, dallying near the gate. If anyone had seen anything strange it would be Thomas. The boy was an invisible sentinel, always observing without being seen. He was simply part of the background.

"Morning," Rackem said.

Thomas scrambled to his feet, brushing dust off his trousers. "Greetings, sheriff. What can I do ya for?"

"Just got a few questions, if that's alright."

"Course."

"Good lad. You were part of the search effort last night, correct? You went with the other men into the southern forest?"

"Yar, so I did." Thomas spat. "Didn't find nothing. Rocks and brush, trees and birds. Seent a few deer tracks. That's about it."

"How late did you boys search?"

"Till about eight, I wager, seeing as I got home around ten. It was past dark when we quit. Them woods get awful spooky in the night, sheriff. I doubt any boy in his right mind would dare enter 'em, never mind go exploring in 'em."

Rackem nodded. He had thought the same thing. "Good of you to lend a hand."

Thomas stretched his lanky arms and yawned. "Just doing my bit. Y'all haven't found him yet?"

"Afraid not. That's why I'm here, Thomas. Have you seen anything odd in the past few days? Anything weird or out of the ordinary? Perhaps a stranger? Perhaps someone doing something strange?"

Thomas thought, looked around, spat. "Nah, not really. Today's a bit quiet. Can't even hear the birds singing. Oh, and Mrs. Ashberry's been sweeping her porch about nine times a day from what I can count. Not sure how dirty them floorboards get in the space of an hour."

Rackem cracked a smile. "I was thinking the same thing. Is there anything else, Thomas? Anything at all?"

Thomas scratched the fluffy blonde hairs on his chin. "One other thing. But I can't imagine how it relates to the Schmidt boy."

"Try me," Rackem said.

The young man squirmed uncomfortably. "Well, ya see, ever since I was a kid, there's only one time I can remember..." Thomas paused, crinkled his nose like he had smelt shit. "Well, that I can remember hearing my folks doin' it. Ya know, in bed."

Rackem nodded that he understood.

"Anyway, the past two nights it's been non-stop. I'm telling ya, sheriff, non-stop. When I wake up, they're doin' it. When I go home around noon to fix something to eat, doin' it. I get home after dark, doin' it."

"That doesn't sound like a cause for concern," Rackem said. "Stanley and Lucile are man and wife in the eyes of God, and as such, have the God-given right to lay in bed together."

"Yar, so they does. But it's not just the doin' it, sheriff. It's the how. It's the noise they make, like squealing pigs. I can hear my da gruntin' and cursin', using words I ain't never heard before—words I ain't willing to repeat. And ma, well, she's in there screeching as if he's killin' her. I was concerned at first, ya know. I thought something terrible was happening. But I seent em after, all sweaty and grinning, and I suppose all is well. It's just odd, sheriff. All my years I ain't never heard nothing like it."

Thomas stared at the barren road with haunted eyes. "The worst of it was last night, after searching for a lost boy who might well be dead and seeing the sadness in poor Lani Schmidt's eyes. Well, they went home and done it louder and meaner than any time before. I mean it, sheriff. It was plain rude. Something the Devil would do, ya know."

The sheriff was thinking. He slid his tongue over his teeth. "When did you say this strangeness started?"

"Two nights back, I reckon," Thomas said. "I guess it started the same night little Johnathon went missing."

The same night Rackem had opened his box. It was enough to make him wonder. Johnathon missing, Lani gone mad, Mrs. Ashberry acting out of sorts. And now Stanley and Lucile practicing some form of heathenistic sex. Rackem prayed it had nothing to do with his drunken excavation. He was sure these things were only coincidences.

Rackem thanked the boy, told Thomas, "I best set off now," and started down the road with a lot of crazy ideas in his head.

Thomas called after him, "Where ya off to?"

"Your house," Rackem said. "I'd like to hear the racket for myself."

"Oh, you'll hear it alright, sheriff. Don't say I didn't warn ya."

6

It was not far to the southern rim of Emmert, where Thomas lived with his parents. Rackem first passed through the town's busiest strip, finding it odd that no one was outside. It was a wide dirt road flagged by houses and shops. Most were cute three or four-bedroom abodes painted white or beige, baby blue or a dark shade of maroon. All were curtained by a short fence, the colors matching the homes. Many had extensions built onto them where tradesmen went about their work.

One example was Logan Reitner's ironworks: an open-air workshop with a roof and a chimney, an anvil and rusted tools hung on the walls and a large furnace that could be seen from the road. Logan was the closest thing to an artist in Emmert, and it showed in the unique design of his house. He had installed a massive front window with the glorious image of The Virgin Mary etched perfectly on its surface. As Rackem passed it, he wondered if the interior was just as eccentric.

Across the street from Logan's shop was the general store. It was titled Carlos O'Brian's Goods and Services, though Carlos didn't offer a single service other than goods. The shop was closed when Rackem rode by, but on an average day there would be a heavy flow of foot traffic and a congregation of men lounging on the stoop, smoking pipes and gossiping.

Farther down the way, Rackem passed The Goodman's Tannery and Mr. Beucanon's two story mansion where he lived with his wife and huge litter of children, the tall silo behind his estate. Then he went by Mrs. Henley's school for children and the picturesque orchard beside it, Pastor Marble's church, and the Ringall's residence. Dun Ringall acted as Emmert's doctor, and his wife, Maria, as his assistant.

Rackem thought about how different Emmert was from other cities. Emmert did not function like Cincinnati,

Fort Boise, or one of the Spanish towns in the Southwest. There were no saloons, no brothels, no hotels. The commerce was shared amongst the townsfolk—goods for goods and service for service. People were kind, courteous, and respectable. There had not been a quarrel in twenty years. Not one drop of blood ever spilled. Perhaps that was the reason Rackem was so bothered by recent events. With the theft of Talbert's son, the unexpected opening of his crate, and the most ominous of auras descending on the town, God only knew what was in store for Emmert.

7

Muffled cries of intimacy penetrated Rackem's ears long before he reached the Weathers' property line. It was as if a hushed moan had been suspended in the air. It gave the initial impression of bawdy windchimes. Rackem halted his horse in the road and listened. There was no other sound, just the faintest whisper of love.

The Weathers lived in a fair tale home. Rackem sat his horse outside the sunny fence and looked in at the pleasant yard. It was serene and beautiful. Vivid butterflies and fat bumblebees hovered around beds of multi-colored flowers. A garden, ripe with tomatoes and juicy red strawberries, stretched the length of the home beneath bright yellow shutters. A small pond glistened in the sunlight, a reading bench unoccupied at its edge.

The image of tranquility was tarnished by the vulgar sounds resonating from within the Weathers' house. As Rackem entered the domain of butterflies and flowers, words became audible alongside the increasingly violent racket of sex—utterances that Rackem had not known to escape human lips. It was enough to make him pause and cover his own mouth, cross his heart and grumble forgiveness from God.

Rackem heard Stanley Weathers denounce his wife as a dog, a witch, and a harlot. Fire and brimstone spewed from Stanley's mouth and tainted the whimsical atmosphere of his property. It seemed that his wife was guilty of many sins, and that Stanley was forced to chastise her for them, apparently striking her with a whip. It was vile and without taste, and Rackem flinched each time he heard the sting of leather against Lucile's flesh.

Rackem moved closer and Lucile's voice became perceptible alongside her husband's. It was equally crass and equally depraved. She cursed Stanley for his brutality, using slurs that Rackem thought only muttered in the most nefarious of saloons in the most godless of towns. Lucile also slandered the name of God. She declared him a fool and demanded to be brought to the ruin of Sodom, then begged to be reprimanded and punished for her position as Satan's filthy whore.

It was too much for Rackem. It made him ill. He banged on the door loud enough to wake the dead. Inside, the voices hushed. He dug his pouch of tobacco from his duster and rolled a cigarette while listening to someone scurry through the house. He was done and smoking by the time Stanley opened the door...

In nothing but his trousers. Sweaty and panting and his hair tousled, a milky juice flowing down the scruff of his flabby chest.

"Howdy, sheriff," Stanley said. His eyes gleamed with impish delight. "What can I do ya for?"

"Are you drunk?" Rackem asked.

"Beg yer pardon?"

Rackem leaned as close as he dared to the buffoon and sniffed him. He stank, but not like booze. Whatever foul odor seeped from Stanley's gross skin was unknown to Rackem.

"Is there a problem?" Stanley asked. He looked amused, not the slightest bit concerned.

"Are you a butcher, Stanley?"

"Wha?"

"A butcher. Do you slaughter pigs?"

Stanley laughed. "Nah, course not."

"Then why does it sound like you are? Why can I hear the sound of squealing pigs from the road?"

Stanley howled and held his gut. "Aw, hell. It's just me and Lucile in here, Rackem. We ain't hurting nobody. Last I checked, what a man and wife does in their home is their own business, according to God."

Rackem wanted to put his cigarette out in Stanley's eye and snuff the smile from his lips. He settled for blowing smoke in his face instead.

"Sure," Rackem said, "what you and Lucile do is your own business, no matter how lewd. But the instant it leaks onto my road it becomes my business. Tell me, Stanley, what do you reckon Mrs. Oswald would think if she happened by with her daughter and got an ear full of your profanity? You reckon she'd laugh it off and go home? I don't. I'd bet my bottom dollar she'd turn around and head straight for my office to lodge a complaint."

"We'll be sure to keep it down," Stanley said. But there was nothing apologetic or remorseful in his tone. He sounded annoyed, impatient and eager for Rackem to leave so he could return to the bedroom.

Rackem didn't know what else to say. He glared at Stanley below the brim of his hat and tried to think of something more, something else to criticize him for. What kind of demon tells his wife, *"Stick your finger in my ass, you fucking bitch."*?

Stanley, apparently. A good church-going man demanding his wife to finger him, calling her a bitch. It was too much for Rackem. Thomas had been right. Stanley and Lucile were in the Devil's playground.

"If that'll be it..." Stanley was anxious to get back at it.

Rackem ground his teeth. "Yeah, that's it. Keep it down. And keep God's name off your tongue."

Stanley nodded and went to close the door. As he did, Rackem got a clear view past the bulb of Stanley's gut and into the dimness of his home, down a hallway and into a bedroom. He saw Lucile there, leaning casually against the doorframe. She was nude, pale, posed erotically. A yellow bonnet rested on her head and its strings dangled between her breasts. She waved at Rackem, then the door slammed shut and she was gone.

Rackem walked back to his horse burdened by confusion. He had known the Weathers since Thomas was a pup, fifteen years past. Rackem had never known them to be so vicious, so appallingly deviant. What the heck had gotten into those two? Lord Jesus, what had gotten into his town? It was as if in evil fog had rolled into Emmert, corrupting all it touched. Rackem had seen it clear in Stanley's horny eyes, in Lucile's nudity, in Lani's madness.

And now Rackem really did wonder if something sinister had washed ashore on the eventide two nights past, that old, malignant force reawakened.

8

Talbert marched through his pasture, past Fiona and Daisy, the grazing cows. He was infuriated with his wife. Johnathon's disappearance tortured him to no end, yet Talbert had not broken down and gone looney. No, Talbert was going to do something. He had dreamt of the woods and the woods was where he went. Through the pasture and down the hill, into the great grove of the southern forest.

Talbert entered the wild domain with a sense of urgency. He hurried past the boundary of tall pines and into the shade where it was cooler. He hastened through perpetual twilight of the forest, sunlight falling through the canopy of leaf and pinecone indiscriminately.

No one in Emmert had much business in the woods. The men came sometimes to fell trees and haul timber to be used in construction, but no one ever ventured into the forest for fun. It was a creepy place. It was why the men went in groups when they cut wood.

They were paranoid of witches, of Indians and superstitious curses.

Talbert was too gung-ho to be worried about fairy tales. He called out, "Johnathon. Johnathon, where are you?" and paused to listen, hearing nothing but the birds chirping in the branches and the rush of water from somewhere beyond.

He called out every few seconds, then waited with his heart tight in his chest for a response. None ever came, and after walking a considerable distance, Talbert became lost in a labyrinth of giant trees with mushrooms blooming from their trunks and moss creeping up the length of them. In fact, moss was everywhere. The entire forest floor was a layer of soft green moss, red dust where dead trees had turned to mulch. There were a few short, droopy saplings, but not many. The trees were large. Many looked to have been split in two by bolts of lightning, and many more were centuries old and boasted impressive caves in their roots where the wind had tried to uproot them. Talbert inspected these dugouts, hoping one concealed his son.

None did. He looked in the earthen craters and climbed the sides of small cliffs to see what he could see, but there was nothing but forest, and Talbert was soon so deep in the woods and had lost all sense of direction.

"Johnathon," Talbert called from the crest of a mossy hill. "Johnathon, where are you?"

As with every other time he hollered, Talbert stood totally still and listened. Unlike the other times, a response came from somewhere in the forest. It was faint, but sounded human.

Talbert's heart dropped. He could not believe it. Could it really be Johnathon? Was he trapped out there in the forest, pinned under a fallen tree or his ankle broken and snared by a tangled root? "Johnathon," Talbert hollered, so loud it burned his throat, "is that you?"

Sure enough, a distant shriek carried through the grove.

Talbert broke into a run. He dashed over toppled trees and scrambled over mounds of soggy soil. His boots sank into clumps of moss and his face was assaulted by thin, low-hanging branches.

The cry grew louder the farther he ran, and it soon occurred to him that someone was releasing long, shrill screams. Talbert's own breath was rapid. His chest was on fire. His legs were sore. He swore he would not stop. Not even if God himself materialized before him.

He could see the frontier, the end of the trees. The grass beyond the infantry of pines glowed fierce green and the sun was a blinding yellow. Huffing and puffing, a stitch in his side, Talbert emerged.

And stopped.

He scrunched his face and looked around at the pasture. Why was there a field on the other side of the woods? Talbert knew the southern forest went on for uncountable miles, and that a man could wander them until he shriveled from age. How was it that he emerged in a glimmering meadow? Why did it look so familiar?

The inhuman wail—something torn from a woman giving birth and hurled through the air—reached his ears and forced his feet to move once more. The noise no longer sounded like a lost boy. It sounded more like a woman in a great deal of pain.

Talbert crowned the hilltop and was looking down at his house. *His house.* The house he and Lani had built together. The house that Johnathon had vanished from. He could see Daisy and Fiona grazing, two white and black dots to the south of his home.

Lani! He thought. *It's her voice I'm hearing!*

Again, Talbert was off, bolting down the side of the hill at a madman's pace. But when Talbert reached his home, it was not Lani's glass-breaking screech disrupting the countryside. It resonated from farther afield, at the Roscal's place. The scream was slowing in procession. By the time he jogged around his house and reached the road, it had cut out entirely.

Talbert continued as fast as he could down the dirt road, towards the Roscal's farm.

9

Past noon and Rackem needed a damn drink. His shakes were getting worse. Sweat trickled down the nape of his neck and he shivered, skin cold. It felt like decay, like his body was giving up on him. He had to get his mind of the withdrawal, off Lucile's naked body. Rackem still had a mystery to solve. Half a day and he had uncovered nothing about Johnathon Schmidt.

After the vileness of the Weathers' house, Rackem sought the least scandalous place he could think of. He went to the home of Pearl and Dennis Tanner, the most devout, virtuous, and wholesome people in Emmert. They were the kind of people that Emmert had been built for. Real straight-shooters. They were happily married at seventeen. They had two young sons, both of whom left Emmert three years prior to spread the word of Jesus Christ to the godless Indians in the newly acquired Oregon Territory. The entire family were servants of God.

Rackem found Pearl Tanner in her yard. She was on her knees in front of a flowerbed, humming a gentle tune while inspecting a rose. She had an assortment of flowers in a neat pile beside her. Calla lilies, tulips, daisies, and something pink that Rackem didn't know. She must have been making one of her famous bouquets.

Pearl saw Rackem coming into the yard. "What a wonderful surprise," she said. "If you would do me the kindness of holding on a single moment." Pearl clipped the rose's stem and twirled it in her fingers. "Ah, there we are. Perfect." She stood, brushed her hands on her skirt. "God bless ye, sheriff." She even gave him a small curtsey.

Rackem, though a grim and frequently dour man, could not help but appreciate Pearl's old fashion demeanor and earnest smile. He flashed one of his own, showing Pearl his rotten teeth. "Afternoon, Pearl."

"What brings you to my neck of the woods on such a splendid day?"

Rackem took off his hat. He was sweating horribly. "I wish I could say a friendly visit, yet I can't. It's office business."

Pearl pouted her lips. "Johnathon Schmidt then. I had a feeling."

"Afraid so. I've started an investigation into the boy's disappearance and the rather confounding mystery surrounding it."

"I see."

"Yes. I need to speak with the folk in town to ascertain who's who and what's what."

"Smart thinking."

"That's why I'm here, Pearl. Talbert and Lani have two neighbors, you and the Roscals. I figured to come here first. Neither you nor Dennis have a bad bone between you. I know you'll help if you can."

"Mighty fine of you to say. My husband and I pride ourselves on our integrity, dare I say our righteousness."

"I'd never dispute it," Rackem said.

"Yet I must let you down, sheriff. I have not seen anything of a dubious or sinister nature. I have not glimpsed a bush, bee, nor bird out of place. Everything is as it should be, from what I can tell. God forgive me, but I am privy to no knowledge of misdeed. I can offer no assistance."

Rackem grumbled. He had figured as much. "No need for forgiveness," he said, tugging on the collar of his duster. Though Rackem was in the shade of a blooming oleander tree, sweat ran profuse down his neck. "You're not at fault."

Pearl smiled at him.

"Perhaps I could talk to Dennis."

"No," she said. "My husband is unwell, and is

currently at rest."

"Dennis is sick?"

"Difficult for me to say," Pearl said. "My husband is without symptom. There was a cough for the past two days, but this morning it's gone away. Asides from a lack of vigor, there is not much to suggest illness. Yet my husband remains sick all the same."

"Curious," Rackem said. Now he had a sick man on his hands. A man who had taken ill two days past. Rackem asked, "Have you gone to see the Ringalls?"

"We will not be doing that," Pearl said with utmost certainty, the air of someone above such criminal intent. "My husband is in God's hands and I will not transfer my darling into the grubby paws of some...some two-bit shaman!"

"Course not," Rackem said. He should have known better. Children of God were beyond the blasphemies of science. "I'll pray for Dennis this evening before bed, for his quick recovery."

Pearl bowed to him. "That would be most favorable of you, and much appreciated. Now, if you don't mind--"

A blood-curdling scream crammed Pearl's words back into her mouth, the noise so strident the great oleander tree shuddered and white petals rained onto Rackem's hat.

"Good lord," Rackem said, "that sounded like Emily Roscal."

It came again, the blast of a tortured trumpet, a visceral shriek that shattered the air and made birds vacate trees in a surge of flapping wings.

Rackem was gone before the third scream, sprinting out of Pearl's yard and across the road to the Roscal's farm. Pearl Tanner watched him go, Rackem's dark coat fluttering behind him like the ripped tail of some prehistoric vulture.

CHAPTER FOUR

1

It was early afternoon and Emily Roscal lounged on her back porch, rocking in an old wicker chair and cradling a glass of chilled lemonade in both hands. She was admiring the eastern expanse of her property, vivid green fields and enough ripe apple trees to feed Emmert for ten years. Her vision fell on Angela, her daughter busy chasing the sheep in their pen with her arms outstretched and the fluffy animals reeling every which way and making throaty noises of distress. The child had no intended victim. Angela happily ruffled the first shaggy white coat she got her grubby, nine-year-old paws on.

Emily took a sip of lemonade and sighed. The liquid was cool and the sun was hot. If not for the racket reverberating from Pete's work shed, she would have been content. Emily hated Pete's clang of tools and metal. It was polluting the tranquility of her afternoon, scaring the birds from the trees. Emily was barely able to coalesce her thoughts enough to ponder with a bit of clarity.

She was trying to decide what to do about Pete's peculiar behavior over the last two days. She thought about talking to him about it, then decided it was useless. Pete seemed oblivious to his own bizarre theatrics, which had all started the day of Johnathon Schmidt's disappearance, early in the morning.

2

Pete Roscal was always working on a new project, building

a clever implement for the farm or something of the sort. The previous summer, Pete had unveiled a spectacular rocking horse for Angela, complete with detachable wheels. Thanks to the robust design and the fancy wheels, Angela was able to take her wooden horse, which she named Bella, onto the road and propel herself through the ruts on her own little pony. She was thrilled.

Lately, Pete had begun preparations on a secret project and refused to let Emily know what it was. Pete had gone so far as to purchase a big heavy lock from Carlos O' Brian, then went on to ensure it was bolted tight each time he left the shed, even if just to fetch a pail of water or go to the outhouse. Pete kept the key on a string around his neck and never removed it. Not even when he slept.

Emily did not mind the secrecy. She was anxious for him to be done so she could see it. Emily was tired of helping Pete drag steel bars and ropes and other strange materials to the shed, where Pete hauled them inside and out of sight. A part of her insisted it would be something very special, something just for Emily. Another part of her wondered what he could possibly be using all that metal for.

"Split in two when you see it," Pete had told her. "Might even go blind from the wonder of it."

She hoped so. She hoped it was that amazing. It was not like Pete had a slave girl bound and tied in the shed or anything. It had to be harmless.

The day Pete's unsettling behavior began was the day he started to labor on the mysterious project, commencing work much earlier than usual.

Emily woke without Pete beside her, which was already unusual. She rubbed her eyes and slithered out of bed, sauntered down the long hallway into the kitchen. The sun was not yet a half-dome on the horizon, but the light was intense and Emily had to shield her eyes because it blasted through the window. She found a spot of shade and peeked outside. Sure enough, the glow of a lamp was obvious inside the shed, though soon the sun would defeat its meager aura. For now, the wooden shed was phosphorescent.

When she opened the back door and stepped onto the porch, Pete's handiwork became audible. Emily heard a *twang* that she figured for a saw. Mrs. Roscal thought every metallic noise her husband made was a saw. She went slowly down the stairs, shivering at the unexpected bitterness of the morning, and pulled her nightgown tighter.

The pandemonium blaring out of the shed was loud enough to mask the approach of an elephant, and so Emily came upon the door unnoticed. From within, metal banged and clanked. Wood creaked. Pete's boots thudded against the floorboards. A saw, Emily thought, cut something in half.

Then it stopped—abruptly, a factory silenced.

It was hushed for about a minute, the only sound Pete's creepy breath from inside. Then he spoke. He spoke and his voice was ugly and malformed as though there were nails in his throat.

"Faggots," Pete grumbled. "Whores and faggots. Deplorable cunts. Cunts and runts and skunks. The lot of 'em. Fuckers. Dead fuckers. Rats for traps is what I say. Yup, that's right, traps for rats."

He snickered and went on talking, but the pounding of a hammer covered his scratchy voice and Emily staggered away from the shed, appalled. She retreated into the house and sat confounded at the table until Pete came inside an hour later.

"Good morning, my love," he said, a happy smile on his face as he walked through the door.

Emily whisked across the room to him, stood glowering over the dirty man, black with grease, the hair on the sides of his skull ruffled like a furry crown. "You were up quite early," she said, arms crossed.

"Aye. Woke up with some ideas that couldn't wait."

"What kind of ideas?"

Pete grinned mischievously. "Secret ideas. But it shan't be long till I'm finished. Don't worry. You'll get to see it soon. Angela, too."

Emily frowned. She had been frowning for the last hour and it made her look old, all her wrinkles getting comfortable on her chalky face. "I suppose that's alright." She did not know what else to say. Pete was clearly fine. Not deranged or mad. Perhaps his monstrous utterings were a kind of method, a way he worked. Maybe they were none of her business.

"I wish you would tell me now," she said. "I hate waiting."

"Patience is a virtue. Remember that."

Emil made a face. "Fine, but you better be finished soon."

"Yes, soon." He grinned.

"Go wash up now," Emily told him. "I'm about to cook breakfast."

The second instance was later that evening, after dinner.

The day had gone on without further weirdness. Emily spent the afternoon kicking herself for being nosey, wishing she had just stayed in bed. But then, when the chores were done and Angela was fast asleep, it happened again.

Emily was hanging the last of Angela's clothes out to dry, hoping she could finish before it got too cold. The warm air had vanished, the night announcing itself with a bitter winter breeze. She hung Angela's favorite yellow dress on the line and went in, ready for a hot cup of coco, for a quiet sit by the fire. What she found instead was Pete's mutant voice echoing throughout the house.

She followed it to the sitting room and paused in the doorway. There was Pete, hunched before the fireplace with his back to her, rocking on the balls of his feet.

"Burn, churn, urn," he said in that ghoulish tone. "Feed 'em to the fire. Whores. Faggots. Maggots and skinned rabbits."

"Pete!"

He tipped and fell on his side, giggling. "Gosh, Emily, you scared me. You move as silent as the air, I tell ya. I reckon you could sneak up on a jackrabbit."

"What were you saying?" Her arms were crossed. she glared at him.

"Pardon?"

"Just now, before I startled you. What were you saying?"

"Nothing," he said, and the look on his face said he believed it. "I was just warming by the fire. Maybe you heard it crackling."

"Maybe," she said, but Emily knew otherwise. She had heard his goblin accent and his cruel words.

"Everything alright?" Pete asked.

"Sure. Maybe I'm tired from getting up so early. I think I'll retire."

Pete gathered himself and walked over to Emily, gave her a hug and a kiss. "Sleep in if you need it. God knows you deserve it."

She smiled, weakly, and left her husband to his fire and his oddness.

3

The next morning was fine. Not once did Emily catch Pete mumbling or saying something strange. Then Talbert Schmidt showed up, distraught and on the verge of tears. Things changed after that. Pete went out and searched around the property, as he said he would. Afterwards, he confined himself to the shed and Emily did not see him for hours. Not until Sheriff Rackem arrived and asked them to help search for Johnathon.

When they got back to the farm, well after dark, Pete was in no mood at all. He was depressed, it seemed. So was she. Even Angela felt the weight of Johnathon's disappearance. Emily had to speak with her before bed.

"Does this mean Johnathon's dead?" Angela asked, tucked tightly beneath her blanket. "I heard some of the women whisper it."

"No, no." Emily said. "Not at all, sweetness. Johnathon's not dead. He just went away without telling his parents, so we went to look for him. We just want to make sure he's safe."

"But we didn't find him. Doesn't that mean he isn't safe?"

Emily bit her lip. "Not exactly. The truth is we don't know, hun. No one knows where he is."

Angela frowned, deep like her mother. "So, he *could* be dead."

"No. He's not dead. Now go to sleep and don't think about it. Pray to God for his safety."

"Alright." Angela didn't sound satisfied.

Emily kissed her on the forehead. "Goodnight, my sweet child."

"Night mommy."

Emily picked up the oil lamp and held it outstretched as she made her way from Angela's room to her own, and for a third time, she was aghast to find Pete in the middle of a demented rant.

He was knelt by the bed and looked to be praying, but what Pete said was far from any Godly hymn Emily had ever heard.

"Hell's bells, ring-a-ding-dong, all night long," he sung. "Heaven's whistle blows, oh down she goes."

"Pete Roscal!" Emily rushed into the room. "What in the name of Jesus Christ are you doing?"

He smiled innocently up at her. "Sending up a silent prayer for the Schmidt's boy. We failed today, Emily, but perhaps on the morrow someone will find him. All I can do is ask God to keep him safe this night."

Emily stared at him. She wondered if it was her or Pete losing their mind. But no, it couldn't be her. Three times was not a coincidence.

"Can you tell me what you said?" she asked. "What you said to God?"

Pete laughed and rose to his feet. "I don't remember the exact words. Something about bringing Johnathon home safe and sound. Strength for Talbert. Courage for Lani. Not much else."

Emily chewed her bottom lip. "Okay," she said. "Okay."

Emily lay awake next her snoring husband for a long time thinking. She rose twice to check that Angela was still in her bed, just in case.

4

By the time Emily finished her lemonade, she wagered it was close to noon. Angela had tuckered herself out and was laying in the grass. The sheep kept their distance. Pete still mashed away at his mysterious project, the shed a hub of awful racket.

Reluctantly, Emily rose from her wicker chair. She stretched her arms to the sky and yawned, then strolled over to the banister and called to Angela. "Angie, sweetness, come help mommy get dinner ready."

Angela sat up. Her dress was the color of daffodils. The same color as her hair. "Okay, mommy."

Angela plodded forward on her hands and knees, slowly evolving onto her feet. She unlatched the sheep's pen, closing it behind her, and skipped towards the house. Angela's yellow skirt rippled as she went, her white socks drawn up to her knees. She was adorable, the very image of a child of Emmert.

There was an ugly well halfway between the sheep's enclosure and the house, and as Angela came upon it, she noticed the gray shell in a haunting way.

The child stopped mid-stride. She cocked her head sideways and observed the shabby reservoir, as if the most curious insect crawled across its surface. Angela changed course and walked straight for it.

"Hey," Emily said, "leave that decrepit thing alone."

Angela was bewitched. She touched the side of the stone, caressing it gently. The way her eyes were wide and full of wonder—it was uncanny, strange, even supernatural how she peered mystified into the well.

"What are you doing?" Emily said. "Get over here right now, Angela. Quit playing around."

Angela struggled to get up the well's brittle wall. One foot, half her body, a knee, and she was standing on the precipice, looking in.

"Angela! Angela!" Emily was screaming from the porch.

Angela dangled her shiny black shoe over the void as if she might walk on air.

"No, Angela! No!"

Angela moved her other foot. She seemed to float above the well for a split second. Then Angela's pretty face cracked against the edge of the stone and she fell in.

Emily was screaming. She was screaming so loud.

5

Pete Roscal squeezed out of his shed, careful not to let anyone glimpse what was inside. He had with him a crude metal hook and a long length of coiled rope.

Talbert and Rackem watched Pete lock his shed and then trudge across the lawn to the well, a disgruntled dwarf of a man with his face set in an unreadable expression. Neither Talbert nor Rackem knew what to do.

Rackem had gotten there first. He had come into the yard to witness Emily Roscal dive head-first into the well, screaming, "Angela! Angela, my baby!" While she clawed at the air. Rackem had made it to Emily just in time to pull her away from the ugly thing, before she slithered in after Angela and joined her daughter forty feet underground.

Talbert had come sprinting into the yard soon after. His first sight was Emily Roscal face down in the grass, sobbing and tearing up chunks of soil. Rackem panted beside her, his hat lost in the scuffle.

"Get Pete out of that damned shed," Rackem had yelled to Talbert. Somehow, Pete had not heard his wife shrieking, even though her cries had penetrated the very fabric of space and time.

Now Emily stood beside the well crying. Her face was red—eyes, cheeks, nose all flushed. Mucus seeped from her nostrils and stuck to her top lip. She looked sick, the way she teetered on the verge of fainting. Talbert wondered what was worse, a sick wife or a crazy one.

Pete pushed the end of his rope through a loop on the hook's handle and tied it in a knot, thus binding them as a seamstress would bind a needle to a length of thread. It was a crude fishing rod, and Pete balanced it in his palms, as if his hands were scales and could measure the severity of such a grim tool. With a wince, he cast the hook into the well.

There was no sound from the bottom. The splash everyone anticipated never came. The hook must have landed on Angela's body. Talbert sighed and pinched the bridge of his nose. Rackem grumbled and looked over at the apple trees, red fruit littered around their trunks like big, sparkling rubies.

Pete didn't move. He just stood there looking at his feet, the rope loose in his hands. Talbert could hardly imagine his despair.

"Pete," Talbert said, taking a step forward. "If you've not the heart..."

"I'll do it," Pete growled. "Leave me be."

Slowly and with intense discomfort, Pete peered down the well, down the vertical tunnel at the floating body of his daughter. The metal hook laid on her back. Angela floated in the murky water like a bloated corpse in the tub.

Pete couldn't get the hook to go where he wanted it to. The damn thing kept dipping into the water, snagging the fringes of Angela's yellow dress, ripping it. It took a good five minutes for Pete to reel her up. He had one boot against the base of the well, heaving. He pulled and groaned, then the hook let go.

Pete flew backwards and landed on his ass, the rope slack in his fists. Angela's body hit the water with a loud splash.

"God be damned," Pete said. He scrambled to his feet and marched back to the well. Emily shrieked and fell to her knees, hysteric.

Pete cast his line, cursing under his breath. This time, when he looked down, Angela stared back at him. She floated in the shallow of yellow dress and yellow hair like a faded doll in a puddle. Her face was blanched, mouth gaped, eyes open. A gash on her forehead was bright pink.

Pete maneuvered the hook beneath Angela's neck and lifted, making a sort of noose below the girl's chin. He hauled her up, Angela rising like a wet angel towards the light.

Angela's body dragged over the wall and flopped onto the grass. Emily scrambled to the dead child on hands and knees. She cradled Angela's wet head. "My baby. My sweet child, what have you done?"

Angela's response was a sick gurgle, the well water trapped in her lungs bubbling from her mouth. Talbert wanted desperately to help. He wanted to kneel beside Angela and breathe life back into her poor soul. He wanted to squeeze Emily's shoulder and tell her everything would be alright, the woman so heartbroken that it broke his own in turn.

Alas, he could not. Pete loomed over his child and

wife with a look of hot vengeance. It made Talbert uncomfortable. Talbert felt like an uninvited guest who had overstayed his welcome. He wanted to leave. The tragedy of it was too much. Too much and not his.

"We should go," Talbert said to Rackem. "There's nothing we can do for them now except let them grieve."

"You can fetch the pastor," Pete said, his expression twisted in—what? Revulsion? Dismay? Furious anger? "I'd say that's the extent of your ability to help us, sheriff. Fetch the pastor so I can bury my daughter."

Rackem nodded. He had no words to express his sympathy, the sudden and brutal loss of a child. "I'll fetch him," he said. "My condolences Pete, Emily."

"Mine as well," Talbert said. "I wish I knew what to say. The tragedy of it, losing a child. You'll be in my prayers tonight. I can promise you that. Angela, too."

Pete turned and locked eyes with Talbert. There was no life in Pete's gaze. When he spoke, he sounded demonic. "Nothing for you to say, Schmidt. We're paddling the same boat into Hell, you and me, *filled* with the bodies of children."

6

Sheriff Rackem returned to the Roscal's farm an hour later with Pastor Marble slouched on the back of Rackem's horse. The pastor was a feeble, wrinkled old thing, by far the oldest man Rackem had ever seen. It was no wonder he moved across the Roscal's backyard like a grandmother. Rackem walked beside him, both men dour in black. The only color between them was the white collar around Marble's throat.

The pastor paused by the well and gawked into it. "How in almighty God did she fall in?"

Rackem shrugged. "Don't know. I didn't see."

Marble *tsked*. "My, my. Poor lass."

They kept on across the yard, past Pete's work shed, to the southern border of the property where Pete and Emily waited for them below the shade of an apple tree. Pete had already dug a hole. He was leaning on the end of his shovel, its spade stuck in a mound of dirt. Angela's body was wrapped in a white sheet beside the grave, a freshly prepared mummy in wait of its burial.

Pastor Marble swung his head sadly, looking down at Angela's covered remains. "Pity," he said, more to himself. "A pity indeed. There has not been the death of a child in Emmert since poor Mrs. Ashberry's daughter. That was an age ago." He made a *tsk* noise, then asked Rackem, "What of the Schmidt boy? Any sign?"

"No." Rackem shook his head. "We're still looking."

The pastor made another *tsk* and shook his head. "Two children gone in as many days. The calamity of it. I only pray the Lord shelter them and keep them in his divine embrace." His hand raised to the wooden cross hung about his neck. He caressed it habitually. "These are dark times for Emmert. Dark times indeed. We had all better pray for the good Lord to shine his light upon our town once more, before more children are taken by the Devil. God is angry. What else could have delivered us his wrath?"

Rackem had a few ideas. One of them involved a bottle of whiskey and a shovel.

Marble said, "I will say a prayer now for the young girl's soul. Does anyone wish to say a few words before I begin?"

"I love you Angela," Emily said. She tried to say more, but emotion caught in her throat and she started to cry.

Pete grunted, "Go on, pastor."

Marble cleared his throat, opened his bible and ran his finger down the page. "Rest eternal, grant unto Angela, O Lord, and let light perpetual shine upon her. May her departed soul, through the mercy of God, rest in peace, and may she rise in glory. For this we pray through Jesus, our lord, Amen."

    Pete scooped up the body of Angela before Marble had closed his bible. "I'd like to bury my daughter now." He never looked at anyone, just stared at the hole in the ground with an expression of pure horror. Rackem felt bad for him. Pete's whole world had just drowned at the bottom of a well. Pete was about to bury his only child beneath an apple tree.

7

Night in Emmert was sleepless for all its peculiar denizens.

    Pete Roscal spent the midnight hours confined to his shed. He worked until the blisters on his hands burst and bloody puss moistened his palms. He slaved with metal and rusted tools until the memory of his daughter slipped away and his mind became an empty void, his body a brainless machine.

    "Soon," Pete said to himself as he hunkered on the floorboards, marveling at his creations by lamplight. "One day, two days, no more than three. Finally, you will be finished, and I, full of glee." He cackled then, loud enough for Emily to hear from where she lay awake in bed, haunted by the death of her daughter.

* * *

Talbert could not sleep without his wife. He stood in the kitchen and watched Lani through the glass window. She stood in front of the storage shed, ghostly as ever in the moonlight. She had not changed her nightgown since the morning of Johnathon's vanishing. Talbert was used to her spectral form haunting their yard. He was beginning to think of Lani as more of a ghost than as his wife.

   Talbert found himself thinking back to what Pete had said: *"We're paddling the same boat into Hell, you and me, filled with the bodies of children."*

    What had Pete meant by it? Probably nothing. The man was grief-stricken, in absolute tatters at the loss of Angela. Talbert would not be surprised if Pete lost his mind, same as Lani. Talbert had a bad feeling the whole town was set to lose their minds.

* * *

Thomas Weathers lay tormented in his bedroom, which happened to share a wall with that of his parents'. Though it made little difference where Thomas was in his house. The boy strolled room to room, Stanley and Lucile's disturbing cries of pleasure following him everywhere he went. Thomas felt stuck in an asylum.

He stretched out in bed and pressed his palms tightly against his ears, hummed a tune as loud as he dared, but the groans of his father and the vile tongue of his mother were inescapable. Thomas flailed in frustration. He buried his face in a feather pillow and screamed, beat it with his fists. Nothing stopped the torture.

Eventually, Thomas could stand it no longer. Weary and exhausted, he dressed in his warmest clothes and left the house. He hoped to find silence on the Emmert Road.

* * *

Rackem gazed into swirling darkness. He was alone, feverish and sick. His black fur blanket was draped around his shoulders and he shivered beneath it. There was a rattle in his ears, the sound of every whiskey bottle locked up in his office jostling against each other, calling to him. It was maddening. Almost as maddening as his wasted day, a whole day and not one clue, only more lost children. It made Rackem crave the booze even more. He shuddered there in his cellar, pulled the blanket tight around him and let the rattle of those bottles eat him alive.

CHAPTER FIVE

1

Thomas Weathers arrived at his post two hours early. He came around the bend of the Emmert Road, in front of Miss. Huntly's red gate, then onwards past Mrs. Ashberry's quiet residence and the sheriff's house. Thomas wore the same fur vest from the night before. He had yet to take it off. His blonde hair was shaggy from rolling in bed.

Thomas slumped against the thick redwood pillars of Emmert's wall and sighed. He was tired. He had barely slept a wink and dreaded another sleepless night. And now he was too scared to venture out onto the Emmert Road. After what Thomas had seen last night, he was too scared to be out after dark.

Two hours Thomas sat and picked his teeth, waiting for the sheriff to wake up. He needed to tell Rackem what had happened, what he had seen on the road at night. Mrs. Ashberry came onto her porch bright and early with her broom, smiled at Thomas and got to sweeping.

Thomas waited a little longer, then got tired of waiting and went over to knock on Rackem's door. The thing he had seen felt too important to withhold any longer.

Rackem opened his door almost immediately, as if he had been standing on the other side staring out the window. "What?" he said. Rackem did not look well. Dark circles enveloped his eyes and his cheeks were sunken in an obvious way. Thomas thought his bushy beard had grayed significantly in the last twenty-four hours.

"I... I seent..." Thomas was nervous before the sheriff. He was clearly in a foul mood.

"Spit it out," Rackem said. "What do you want?"

"I..." Thomas blinked at Rackem, sweaty in a gray tunic and terribly ugly. He looked like he had scurvy. "I've seent a thing."

Rackem narrowed his eyes at the boy. "What kind of a thing?"

"A thing you 'ought to know about. It's got to do with the Schmidt boy."

Rackem's eyes grew wide. "Wait here," he said, and closed the door.

Thomas sat down on the top step while he waited. Across the street, Mrs. Ashberry leaned over her banister with her giant breasts pushed up nearly to her chin. She watched Thomas intently, a bizarre look in her eye.

The door opened and Rackem took a seat beside Thomas, fully dressed in his grungy duster and wide brim hat. Before he spoke, Rackem took his pouch of tobacco and rolled a cigarette. He could barely keep the leaf in the paper because his hands shook so much.

Rackem lit his cigarette with a match. "What is it then?"

"The other day," Thomas said, "after we had that talk, did you happen by my place?"

"I did."

"What did you hear?"

Rackem frowned. "You know full well what I heard."

"Yar. I reckon I does." Thomas spat over the steps. "Now you know it too."

"What's your point?"

"Well, sheriff, my point is this. You heard it for a minute, maybe two. I've been hearing it for the past few nights. *All night* for the past few nights. I reckon ma and pa ain't been falling into bed—well, ya know what I mean. Going to sleep, that is, until the roosters are waking everyone else up. As you can imagine, sheriff, I ain't been getting much sleep."

"Sure." Rackem blew smoke through his nostrils. "I can see that."

"Well, last night I couldn't take it no more. I went for a walk, ya know, to clear my head. Figured if I went for a stroll down the Emmert Road I could at least get some darn silence. Figured I could get ma's squealing out my head. Anyway, I didn't want to come into town. Can't say why. Just didn't. I unlatched the south gate and went down that a way."

Thomas took a deep breath, ruffled his hair and made a pained expression. "I didn't get far. The sounds faded, praise the Lord, but soon after I seent a thing on the road."

"What thing?" Rackem nearly yelled.

"Well, maybe was a gal, maybe a guy. I can't be sure. It was dark, ya see, and they was wearing a type of coat I ain't never seent before, like a robe with a hood, something out of a book. Anyway, this person looked to have come from the Oswald's property, through the bushes, and we spotted each other once they was in the middle of the road. Let me tell ya, sheriff, it was scary. They looked at me but I couldn't see their face. It was too dark beneath their hood. Too dark on the road for that matter.

"They held a big ol' sac in one hand. Dunno what was in it. If I didn't know any better, sheriff, I'd say they was trying to intimidate me. I guess it worked. They took one step toward me and I was running as fast as my skinny legs would carry me back home. Didn't even shut the gate behind me."

Rackem's cigarette had turned to ash between his fingers. He let it fall to the step. "You're sure it was a person?"

"Sure. I mean, I was real tired. Could have been a

shadow, but I doubt it."

"My god," Rackem mumbled. "Perhaps we do have a lurker in Emmert."

Just then a rider came into view on the Emmert Road, approaching from the south. They passed Logan Reitner's place at a steady gallop. The sound of his hammer ceased as the rider went by. Carlos O'Brian eyed them from where he stood impatiently on his stoop, waiting for his regular customers that seemed to have deserted him. Then the rider was at Rackem's place. He dismounted and left his horse in front of the small stable where Rackem's ebony mare was hitched, then came to stand at the bottom of the porch.

"Howdy, Talbert," Thomas said.

"Good morning, Thomas. Morning, sheriff."

Rackem stood up. "Morning, Talbert. Though it's nearly afternoon. Did you just wake?"

"Aye. I haven't slept this late since I was a boy. You too?"

"Yup."

Talbert shook his head. "It's got to be the stress. It's exhausted us."

Rackem grumbled like he didn't believe it. How could everyone in town be sleeping late?

"I need to speak with you," Talbert said, "it's important."

"I was about to tell you the same thing," Rackem said. "Thomas here saw someone last night. A stranger lurking down near the Oswald's place."

"What?" Talbert freaked out. "A stranger? What stranger?" He grabbed Thomas by his collar and rattled the boy. "Who was it? What were they doing?"

"Let him go," Rackem said.

Slowly, Talbert released Thomas, blinking wildly and shaking his head. "Sorry, kid. I'm at my wit's end. I'm losing it."

"No trouble, Mr. Schmidt. It's understandable,

given the circumstances and all."

"Aye. Now tell me about this stranger, if you would be so kind."

"Course. It was a guy or gal. I'm not sure which. They was in a hood. They was leaving the Oswald's place last night 'round two in the morn. I couldn't see their face." Thomas' own face flushed then. "I kind of ran away."

"That was probably for the best," Rackem said. "The last thing you want is to confront a lurker alone. Never mind in the middle of the night."

Thomas nodded. He still looked bashful.

"Do you know what this means?" Talbert said to Rackem.

"I've got an idea."

"It means Johnathon could still be alive. This prowler might have my boy held up some place. If we set a trap for him tonight, I reckon we could get the truth out of him."

"You reckon he'll come back?" Thomas asked.

"I don't care," Talbert said. "If there's even the slightest chance I can find Johnathon, I'll take it. God be praised!"

Just then another rider came galloping up the Emmert Road at a lunatic's pace. It was Pete Roscal. He rode his horse as though he wished to kill it of exhaustion. He came upon them so fast he had to yank on the reins and his horse reared up and kicked, nearly throwing Pete off its back.

"Hell of a morning, eh sheriff?" Pete said from atop the bewildered animal.

"Beg your pardon?"

Pete spat in the dirt. "You want to know what I woke to this morning?"

Mrs. Ashberry had taken to leaning on her railing, fixed on the commotion. Miss Huntly had come into the street, same as Carlos O' Brian. Logan was out in front of his smithy, covered in soot with a big hammer in his hand. Others, too, watched from windows and front lawns.

"Can you keep your voice down?" Rackem said. "I understand you're grieving, but there is no need for such savage behavior."

"You want to talk about savage?" Pete's face was dark red. "Savage, Rackem, is the man who digs a young girl out of her grave in the middle of the night and slinks off like a god-forsaken witch with her corpse. Would you call that savage? Would you?"

"Hold on a minute," Talbert said. "Someone stole Angela's body?"

"That's right, Schmidt. In the dead of night a goddamned graverobber came into my yard, dug up my daughter's body and took her away. I demand to know who's responsible."

Rackem said, "I'll tell you now, Pete, I'll be looking into that straight away. But screaming about it in the street will do no good. You're only causing a scene." He gestured to the gawkers on the road.

"I don't give a fuck." Slobber flying from Pete's his mouth. "They can look all they want, Rackem. Fuck them. Fuck these people."

Even at such a distance, Rackem could hear the gasp from the crowd. Logan Reitner took a few steps forward, his grip tight on his hammer.

"Go home, Pete," Rackem said. "Cool down. I'll come by soon to investigate."

"Fuck your investigation." Pete spat in the dirt. "I'll find the bastard on my own."

They all watched Pete turn his horse and race back the way he came, nearly trampling Miss. Huntly as he went.

"What a nutter," Thomas said.

"Aye," Talbert agreed, "that's what losing a child will do to a man. I feel sorry for him. I pray that God grants him peace."

Witch Bones

"Forgiving as always, Mr. Schmidt. No surprise coming from you."

"Regardless of Pete's attitude," Rackem said, drawing in close to Talbert and Thomas, "we need to see that grave. If someone did desecrate it, I'd bet the socks off my feet it was the same person you saw last night, Thomas. I bet the sac you saw contained Angela's remains."

Thomas twisted his face in disgust, thinking about that innocent girl's bones stuffed in a crazy man's sac. "Hold on a minute," he said. "I seent em' come from the Oswalds, on the other side of the street. That don't make a lick of sense."

Rackem shook his head. "No, Thomas, it sure doesn't."

2

Talbert and Rackem had saddled up and headed to the Oswald's residence, leaving Thomas alone in the street. Everyone else had gone back about their business, and Mrs. Ashberry had lured Thomas onto her porch. Now she was standing far too close for his liking, almost touching Thomas with her round belly.

"What was all the commotion about?" she asked, chubby cheeks bloated in a smile.

Thomas was not the brightest teenager in Emmert. He gave Mrs. Ashberry all the goods. "There's a stalker on the loose. And last night, someone crept in and stole Mr. Roscal's daughter from the ground. Crazy days in Emmert, I reckon."

"Crazy indeed," Mrs. Ashberry said. "It's a crying shame about Angela. She was such a plump child, such a juicy child. Say, Thomas, are you hungry? I have some freshly baked sweets in the house. You're welcome to come in and have a taste."

"Sure," Thomas said. Thomas loved sweets.

3

Frank and Betsy Oswald were quiet people. They kept to themselves mostly, spending their days tending to the hundreds of tobacco plants in the fields behind their home. They also cared for two dozen chickens, a flock of sheep, six cows, four goats, and an energetic twelve-year-old girl.

It was because of the Oswald's reputation as genial folks, introverted and soft spoken—if not a touch eccentric—that Talbert and Rackem were surprised to come upon their doorstep and behold shouts emanating from within the home. Yet they did not sound angry. Frank and Betsy's words were flung about in an indistinguishable din of panic.

Rackem knocked hard on the door.

It swung open and Frank Oswald stood shirtless and panting in the threshold, a pair of flimsy breeches all that covered his manhood. He looked disappointed when he saw who had knocked.

"Afternoon, Frank," Rackem said.

Frank blinked, confused as if he had just woken up and had no idea where he was. "Afternoon? Say true?" Frank pushed past Rackem and squinted up at the sun. "I'll be darned. It's mid-day already."

Rackem checked his pocket watch. "Twenty after one," he said.

"Twenty past one!" Frank turned and shouted into the house, "Bets, it's twenty past one!"

Betsy appeared in the doorway and wriggled in beside Frank. Both husband and wife had a bad case of bedhead, their matching, shoulder-length hair tangled in knots. "How's that possible?" she asked.

"I don't reckon I know," Frank said. "When's the last time we slept so late?"

"Never. Not once in my whole life have I slept past breakfast. Not once. I'll be gosh darned if we both slept until the middle of the afternoon."

"Hold on a minute," Talbert said. "Have you just

woken up?"

"That's right," Frank and Betsy said, creepily at the same time.

"We fell asleep pretty early," Frank went on, "right after we got wind of Angela Roscal's death. Poor girl. We didn't tell Noel. We didn't want to upset her. The two were friends after all."

"Best of friends," Betsy said. "We put Noel to bed and were quick to follow. It's not often we're awake after dark."

"Nope," Frank said, "not often at all. We woke just now before you knocked to find the sun bright outside our window, groggy as heck."

"That's right," Betsy said. "It felt like we slept an entire week."

"True, Bets. We felt heavier than a sack of rocks. We went into Noel's room to see if she had slept in too, and well... you had best come see for yourselves."

"Come in and look for yourselves," Betsy said, grabbing Frank and clearing the doorway. "Don't bother with your boots. The floor's a heck of a mess already."

Talbert and Rackem exchanged a worried look, then entered the Oswald's home.

They saw the mess right away. Talbert nearly tripped over himself trying to avoid the red footprints scattered by the door. Frank lifted his foot and showed Talbert. It was wet with blood. "I stepped in it," he said, as if that explained anything. "Now hurry, fellas, this way."

Frank led them down a short hallway, the red footprints like a murderer's sick trail in and out of their house. "In here." Frank gestured to the bedroom at the end of the hall. "It's a darned bloodbath."

Talbert and Rackem got as far as the room's threshold before both men grimaced and covered their noses. It smelt like wet dog and warm death. There was a shredded brown cadaver on Noel's bed, baby blue sheets awash in rusty stains. Blood was splattered on the wall, the window, the dresser. A pool of it had formed beside the bed and it rippled each time a droplet fell from the bedframe.

"Lord in Heaven," Talbert said, crossing his heart with his spare hand while still pinching his nose. "What's happened here?"

Frank said, "Looks as though an eagle got loose in the house and tore poor old Edgar apart with its talons."

"Some sort of bird, anyway," Betsy said.

"But where is Noel?" Talbert asked.

"Don't know." Frank shrugged "Maybe the eagle got her."

"Don't be daft," Betsy said, then turned her attention to Talbert. "Frank does speak true, Mr. Schmidt. We have no idea where Noel is. We had just walked into her room and started screeching when you knocked on the door. You might have heard us."

"We did, but I didn't think..."

"No," Frank said. "Why would you?"

"Window's locked from the inside," Rackem said, scrutinizing the latch. "Whoever did this entered through the front door."

"Nope," Frank said. "I unlocked the door to let you fellas in. No other door but the one in the back, and I *know* that's locked."

"Locked up tight," Betsy said.

Talbert didn't get it. How could Noel have gotten out of the house? Could she walk through walls? Could Johnathon walk through walls?

"Can we talk about this in the hall?" Rackem asked, abandoning the gore show. He had felt queasy all morning and the sour odor of dog meat was making him want to puke.

They gathered in the hallway and Rackem said to Talbert, "I reckon Johnathon's room looked more or less the same, minus a dead dog."

"Aye, so it did. The window was locked. I don't remember about the front door, but I do remember thinking how strange it was, like Johnathon had gotten up to use the outhouse and never came back."

"You think it's the same person?" Frank asked.

"Of course." Rackem's tone was sharp. "How many kidnappers do you wager live in Emmert?"

"Probably just the one," Betsy said.

"Yeah, just the one," Frank echoed.

"That's right. Just one person. One person too clever for their own good. Whoever we're dealing with has managed to enter two homes without opening a single door, then vanish without a trace. They're capable of tearing a dog to shreds and snatching children from their beds without raising alarm. The part that scares me the most is people seem to be sleeping longer than they have any right to be, as if they're under a spell."

Frank and Betsy scratched their arms nervously. What Rackem said made it seem like the culprit was a spook, sneaking through walls and abducting children. It made the superstitious country folk uneasy.

"A witch?" Frank blurted. "Is that what you're trying to say, sheriff, that a darned witch is stealing our kids, walking through walls and carving up hounds?"

"I don't know," Rackem said. The sheriff had a terrible fear of witches. He hoped it wasn't true. He prayed to God it wasn't true. "Could be someone with a criminal past, a good hunter, maybe a hermit living in the woods outside town."

"Could it be an Injun?" Betsy asked.

"Could be," Rackem said, "though kidnapping isn't common with normal tribes. Might be an outcast, some dejected Indian hiding in the woods."

"It doesn't matter." Talbert had his arms cross, frowning at the red footprints on the floor. "We'll find out for ourselves tonight. We're going to catch this sun of a gun."

"How's that?" Frank asked.

Betsy gave Talbert a quizzical look. "Yeah, Talbert, how's that?"

Rackem grumbled. "Might as well come with us, Frank. Talbert and I need to stop by the Roscal's place and follow up on something. We'll explain on the way. You can explain it to Betsy later."

Frank turned to his wife. "That alright with you?"

"It's alright with me if it's alright with you. I'll wait here in case Noel comes home."

"Okay," Frank said, "I'll be back after we get to the bottom of this whole mess. I'm going to find our daughter. No bastard's taking our girl from us. I can promise you that."

Talbert cringed. He had said the same thing to Lani three days ago.

4

The story of Thomas Weathers and a hooded figure in the night was retold during the short trip from farm to farm. A few questions were asked by Frank and answered by whoever knew them. The idea of an ambush was broached. When Frank asked where, Rackem asked him a simple question in return.

"Who's lost their children, Frank?"

"Talbert and myself," Frank said. "We are the two southernmost farms in town. After us is the Roscals, but they've already lost Angela, God bless her innocent soul. Next up the road are the Tanners, yet their kin are grown and gone."

"That's right," Rackem said. "Keep following the trail. Who's next?"

"Well, the Henley's have two daughters and a son. The Masons have two boys. Their farms are across from one another. It could be either family who's next on the kidnapper's list. How will we know which house to watch?"

"We watch them both," Talbert said. He was critical in his resolve. Damnit, he needed his boy back!

Frank frowned. "We'll need more men if that's the case."

"Aye," Talbert said, "and with a lunatic on the loose, I'd wager the people of Emmert are keen to stop him."

They were on the Roscal's property now, the sun blazing at its highest point, ready for its decline below the western world, that new and frightening land of unknown curses, witches in the woods and savage tribes of cannibals. Though no one would have guessed it for how green and bright the place was, the sweet smell of spring in the air. No one would have guessed a girl's bones had been dug out of her grave twelve hours ago.

Rackem rasped his knuckles against the Roscal's door and the three men lingered on the porch for an uncomfortable amount of time before Emily opened it. She looked defeated, positively beaten by the death of Angela. "Good morning," she said. Her voice was hollow.

"Afternoon, Mrs. Roscal," Frank said. He removed his hat and held it to his heart. "I'm so sorry for your loss. You have mine and my wife's deepest sympathy."

"Thank you." Emily's voice came out empty, deprived of life.

"Is your husband home?" Rackem asked. "He out back in that shed of his?"

"He's gone. He went off looking for Angela's body. Someone's taken her. Dug her right out of the ground."

"That's why we're here," Rackem said. "We want to help."

Her eyes floated listlessly between them, lethargic, Emily's demeanor that of a despondent woman crippled by tragedy. "Okay."

Her sadness made Rackem's heart hurt. "We're

going to look at the grave," he said. "Is that alright?"

"Okay." And Emily closed the door without another word. They could hear her feet shuffle over the floorboards inside. Her misery made Talbert think of Lani. He wondered what his crazy wife was doing.

5

At the southern border of the Roscal's property, beneath the shade of an apple tree, Frank, Talbert, and Rackem stood shoulder to shoulder and inspected Angela's ravaged grave.

The neat hole Pete had dug the day before, then filled in and smoothed over, had been defiled, apparently by a wild animal. The soil was scattered all over the place, as if Angela had reanimated and clawed her way out of the ground. There were no shovel marks, no tool left as evidence. The small white cross at the grave's head had been snapped in two and covered with dirt.

Rackem hunkered beside the grave. There were claw marks in the dirt and Rackem traced them with his finger. "Whoever did this did it with their hands," he said. "These are finger marks. Thin, thin fingers. If they were in sets of three, I'd dismiss this as a wolf, but each set has four. Four fingers." He pointed to the grave's edge. "See that?"

"Aye," Talbert said.

"Looks like claws," Frank said, "like whatever tore apart poor Edgar. This guy must be one sick son of a beast."

Or girl, Rackem thought.

The sheriff stood up, made a slow circle around the grave and inspected the ground, then expanded his search, grumbling as he wandered in a wider and wider loop. Talbert and Frank stepped out of his way and watched. "Nothing," Rackem said. He went and checked beneath a few other trees, hunkered and brushed the dirt with his hands. "I see no tracks. Nothing. I wonder where Pete's gone. He's got nothing to follow."

"Most likely storming through the woods," Talbert said, "shouting at the crows. Pete was in an awful huff when we saw him last. He's out for vengeance."

Rackem nodded, flicked his cigarette in the empty grave. "I hope he's alright," he said. "Pete's a good man. He's just been dealt a horrible hand."

6

Pete Roscal followed a trail of footprints from Angela's place of interment into the fields behind Talbert Schmidt's house. The imprints were obvious in the packed dirt below the apple trees, small and close together, and in the moist fields were even easier to spot, like whoever left them had stomped their feet into the grass on purpose. The tracks led due south, across Talbert's pasture, over a hill, and down into the dark woods.

It was cool inside the grove. Pale, bony branches obscured most of the sunlight. It was silent, too. Anyone hidden amongst the brush and saplings and tangled roots would have heard Pete's insane hollering from a mile away, for he marched through the twilight like a bald, stunted bear in search of food, foul of temper and bawling in anger.

"Come out, you rotten scoundrel," Pete roared down shadowy lanes of firs and pines. "I know you're out here," he declared to the decomposing logs. "You whoreson," he exclaimed, and only the crows on their branches heard him.

The graverobber's trail was more difficult to follow in the woods. Here and there was a snapped twig or some ruffled leaves, the faintest print in a clump of muck. Pete found himself sniffing about aimlessly until something caught his eye, a dimple in a patch of moss or a scuff mark in the soil. Then he would raise his fist and cry out, "Got you, you bastard," and hurry in that direction until again he was lost.

Pete's feverish pursuit took him deeper into the

forest than he could have possibly known. He wound up in an area devoid of light or warmth, a place creeping with shadow, where an icy wind rattled branches and cast dead leaves dancing in miniature storms. It appeared to have no source, this wind, and the screech of it a thousand voices.

A bitter chill settled in Pete's bones. His rage cooled and without it came disheartenment. He wandered sullen through the darkening woods, the thief's trail long lost, and tried to remember why he had acted so psychotic, so angry and so cruel.

He could not recall.

The previous days seemed far away and inconsequential in the depths of the creepy forest. The shuddersome feeling of a hundred watching eyes made it impossible for Pete to concentrate. He peered in brambles and thickets, down shaded alleys of redwood trees, for anyone who might be lurking in the woods. He never found a soul, only the blur of some vague figure scurrying alongside him through the trees. Pete could never distinguish who or what it was.

He entered a realm of close-knit trees that were skinny and twisted and whose branches drooped like vines, their bark gray like molted flesh. From somewhere in the gloom an owl hooted, but Pete was damned if he could see anything through the tangled foliage.

Pete would have turned back if he wasn't so stubborn. He had gone into the woods to find Angela's body, and that was what he intended to do, even if Pete had to stay in the forest all night, shivering and mad with paranoia. Even when the ground became soft and turned to mud, when brown, stagnant bogs made their appearance and he began to wade through a foggy swamp, Pete pressed on.

He found himself wading through sinkholes, scrambling over floating logs and leaping between dry mounds of moss. There was no obvious route to take. It was all the same. Pete was lost in an everlasting marsh. No choice but to continue, to find whatever sick freak called this place home and get his daughter's body back.

Then came the fog, a nebulous billow that covered Pete's boots, wispy tendrils rising from the cloud like the arms of a hundred ghosts, all wanting to drag Pete into a murky quagmire. Still, he persevered. He struggled onward until he teetered over the edge of a steep hill, its precipice invisible beneath the fog, and tumbled down through wet leaves and slick mud.

Pete tumbled all the way to the bottom and splashed into a puddle of muck, nasty water sloshing into his mouth and eyes. He lifted himself up and sat on his ass, stretched his legs in the slush. "Fuck." Wiping mud off his face and spitting it out. "I can't believe this shit." He scooped gunk from his eyes. "Damned forest." And flicked it on the ground. "If there were ev--"

That was when Pete found Angela. The horror of it sucked the air from his lungs.

Before him loomed two menacing trees of the purest black he had ever seen. Their branches were few but strong, muscled with knots. The gnarled limbs of one sinister tree reached for those of the other and made a wreath of ebony bark between the two. And suspended in the middle of the dark timbers was the naked and mutilated corpse of Angela Roscal. She was bound to either trunk by steel wire manacled around her wrists and ankles in barbaric coils, pulled tight so her limbs were overextended. An incision ran from Angela's sternum to pubis and revealed a hollow pocket where the girl's ribs had been pulled apart and her organs harvested. The folds of skin dangled like pastel sails in a dead wind.

Pete vomited on himself. There was his daughter, taut between two black trees like a child Christ on an invisible cross.

Angela's head twitched. The droopy skin around Angela's empty eye sockets moved. There was something in her skull. A rodent's furry head forced its way from her eye hole and sniffed the cold night air. It was a bat. It crawled down Angela's cheek while a second bat squirmed from Angela's other eye socket. They squeaked and flew away into the night.

Now Angela's body was convulsing. A horde of bats erupted from the void in her torso and exploded through her eye sockets, funneled out of her toothless mouth and took to the skies, blotting out the moon with their mangy black wings.

Pete rolled psychotically in the mud.

CHAPTER SIX

1

Sundown on the Emmert road and Sheriff Rackem was in a foul mood. He hadn't had a drink in two days. His irritation was at fever pitch.

He grit his teeth and checked out the rag-tag bunch of farmers and merchants he had spent the afternoon gathering. They had all come easily enough. They were good folk, Christian folk. Everyone was eager to help Rackem catch the bandit, to protect their own children. Some were even armed. Abernathy Congar had a damn scythe in his hands. The silly old fool was more likely to chop off his own head than the head of the kidnapper.

Patty Mason stormed up to Rackem and pointed her beaky nose at him. "What is the meaning of all this? Why is Talbert Schmidt knocking on my door this late in the afternoon? Why is he telling me stories about kidnappers and prowlers? Why does he insist on guarding my home? I know his boy is gone, sheriff, and I am sympathetic. But this is a tad much, don't you think? As if someone would come into *my* home and take *my* boys. Preposterous is what that is. Preposterous, I say."

Patty's voice was making Rackem's head hurt. She wouldn't shut up. All he wanted was to protect her children.

"Have you been drinking?" Patty leaned close and sniffed Rackem's collar.

"No." He cleared his throat. "Not today."

She narrowed her eyes at him anyway. "Then this idea is a sober one. You must be mad, sheriff, to bring all these people here. Why in the name of God does Frank Oswald have a pitchfork? Does he think the British are coming? My God, sheriff, you have assembled an angry mob in front of my home. This looks like the rabble before a witch hunt."

Witch. The word made Rackem flinch. He opened his mouth to argue with Patty, but she was right. He had brought a peasant army down the Emmert Road. Logan Reitner had his big hammer with him, as if to cave someone's skull in. Carlos O' Brian and Conner McBridge had wood axes rested on their shoulders like muskets. They looked like peasants set on burning down mills and slaughtering a medieval monster.

"I guess it does look that way," Rackem said.

"You bet it does." Patty crossed her skinny arms over her chest. "That's exactly how this looks. Talbert claims everyone is here to protect us. He says the same man who stole his son is coming tonight. He says the kidnapper is after us next. Either us or the Henleys. Now I don't know what kind of fairytale Talbert Schmidt has weaved for you, but there are no kidnappers in Emmert, sheriff. Not here. Not in our town."

Rackem was out of patience. He could not endure Patty's squawking any longer.

"Are you daft?" he said. "Two children have been taken, Patty. Their names are Johnathon Schmidt and Noel Oswald. They were poached from their beds in the dead of night, unbeknownst to anyone until the morn. Speaking of *dead*, I watched Pete Roscal reel his daughter's wet corpse out of a well like she was a trout on his fishing line. That makes a total of three children. Three missing or deceased. Does it not occur to you that someone is responsible?"

Patty put her hands on her hips and huffed. "Rude." Then stormed off towards her house, leaving

Rackem with a brain ache, wondering when everyone in Emmert had gotten so... goddamn strange.

Talbert and Patty's husband, Darrel Mason, caught the disgruntled woman halfway down the lane. After a brief discussion, Patty continued to her house and Talbert and Dennis approached the sheriff.

"She give you a hard time?" Darrel asked. "Patty's got a mouth on her that just won't quit. It's enough to drive the Devil back to Hell with his hands over his ears."

"She's just worried," Rackem said. "Women worry different than men."

"Aye," Talbert said, "that they do." He looked down the Emmert Road and thought of Lani, what madness she was about now.

"Patty's going to get the boys ready, sheriff, Sir," Darrel said. "I figure we'll sleep in the parlor together, us and the kids. I'll bring extra wood to keep us toasty and safe through the night, though I doubt I'll sleep. Not with this madness going on. My oldest boy may not either. I've taught him too well, so I have. If he does close his eyes, it won't be till the wee hours of the morning."

Darrel lowered his voice and leaned in close to Rackem. "I almost hope this son of a dagger tries something with me. I've got my old service rifle prepped and waiting. I'll blow a hole through the bastard like I did those godless Injuns."

"Don't miss," Rackem said. Absently, he reached inside his duster and stroked the grip of his pistol. "I know I won't."

Darrel nodded. "Best get back now. I want the hearth hot and the wood stacked high before night's dawn." He looked at the grove of trees on the western edge of the road. The light was dim through their leafy branches. "Less than a half hour by the look of it."

"I want Frank Oswald in there with you," Rackem said, "in case you do fall asleep. I'm not sure what good his pitchfork will do, but at least his voice will rouse the rest of us."

"Aye," Talbert said, "Frank is just as bent on catching this fiend as I am. Neither of us will be sleeping tonight."

Darrel nodded, sucked on his teeth. "I'll get him now."

He walked over to where Frank Oswald leaned on the dull end of his pitchfork and conversed with Abernathy Congar. Darrel took him aside and they spoke for a minute, then retreated across the street and up the path that led to Darrel Mason's home. Abernathy was left to himself and he joined Carlos O' Brian and Conner McBridge in a loud discussion about the Northern Paiute Indians, who lived south of Emmert in the canyon lands, and how everything was their fault.

"Is this it?" Talbert asked Rackem.

"Yeah. Too many men and we're likely to scare off the abductor. That would be bad. Besides, half the people I've gathered are just as inclined to snore as they are to keep watch. Better we rely on just a few."

Talbert said, "My father always taught me one good hand is better than two tied behind your back. I reckon there's sense enough in that." He beamed at the memory of one of Eli Schmidt's life lessons—but his smile quickly faded. Emmert was a cold place that day. There was something in the air that sucked even the slightest warmth from every man's soul.

"Where's Thomas?" Talbert asked. "I'd have thought him eager to be here."

"Don't know. I haven't seen him since this morning. I went to his house but no one answered. It was quiet. Real quiet." Rackem hadn't even heard the blasphemous love cries from Stanley and Lucile when he had knocked on their door.

Just then the sun slipped below the Earth's mantle and a cold darkness shrouded the Emmert Road. The babble ceased. Men shivered and pulled tight their jackets. They looked warily at the shadows that broke free of their daylight prisons, beginning to creep about the trunks of trees and the fringes of shrubs. Down the road, an obscure traffic of shades crossed from one side to the other.

"Sun's down," Rackem said, and all the men looked suddenly nervous. "Gather 'round. I'll explain your posts."

2

The children's names were Joel, Nancy, and Caitlyn. Those were the Henley's brood. The Mason's sons were named Danny and Samwell. Danny was sixteen and Samwell was eleven. Danny did not want to sleep. As the darkness made black the parlor's only window and a bitter chill filled the room, he vowed to his father, "I'll stay awake all night, pop. I ain't going to let some kidnapper take me or Danny. If he tries to come in here, I'll show him a thing or two."

Darrel smiled and ruffled the kid's hair. "I bet you will, pal. Tell you what, pull up some chairs real close to the fire so we can stay awake, let your mother and your brother get some rest. Samwell's got a few years to go before he's as tough as you are."

"Alright." Danny fetched two chairs from the dining table and dragged them across the floor to the fireplace.

Patty glared at them from the other side of the room, where she was busy preparing their beds. "You're not thinking about staying up all night, are you? I sure hope not. If you want to be a dolt by the fire, Darrel, that's your business, but leave Danny to his rest."

"He's sixteen," Darrel said, rolling his eyes. "If the boy wants to sit by the fire with his father, leave him be. It's not every day we wait for a villain to knock on our door."

Patty narrowed her eyes, then turned back to the

bedsheets and mumbled quietly to herself.

Frank Oswald entered the room, his pitchfork left in the hallway. "Could I trouble you for some coffee?" he asked. "I've never stayed up the whole night through before, and a cup of coffee would be mighty helpful."

"Some for us, too," Darrel said, watching the flames lick the mantle.

Patty sighed. "Finish with these sheets and crawl into one," she said to young Samwell. Then she walked straight past Frank and into the hallway. "Come, I'll make your coffee."

While Frank sat in the Mason's hallway and sipped his coffee, listened to the hushed whispers of Darrel and his son, Abernathy Conger and Carlos O'Brian were not so lucky, nor as comfortable.

Carlos was in the Mason's backyard, underneath their porch. Moonlight peeked through spaces between the boards and sticks poked him in the back. He complained about the filthy detail he got picked for, and how his good trousers were now stained with dirt. He spent the first hour of his watch debating if he should go back home.

Abernathy was in front. He had chosen a clump of tomato plants to disguise his gangly body inside of, and was spread out amongst them, his scythe nearby in the soil. He was asleep before anyone else.

Across the street, Joel, Nancy, and Caitlyn were in bed, unaware of the potential danger. They slept in their own room, in their own beds, with Logan Reitner and his huge hammer standing guard outside their door. Once the children were asleep, Retha Henley crawled into bed with Nancy, her youngest, and held her tight.

Clyde Henley imitated his neighbor. He sat close to the hearth and the hungry flames painted his rigid face orange and red. He held an iron fire poker with both hands and listened to every creak and every groan his house made, cocking his head sideways whenever something odd penetrated his ears.

In the Henley's backyard, Conner McBridge sat on a stump behind the shed and leaned forward on his axe, eyes set on the back stoop. Mr. Ringall, Emmert's only doctor, patiently lingered inside the stables, the whole front of the house in plain view.

On the darkened Emmert Road, Talbert Schmidt and Sheriff Rackem spoke in whispers.

"I doubt they'll come now," Rackem said. "It's too early. It's dark, but it's early. In two more hours, I'd guess. Between midnight and three o'clock."

"The witching hour," Talbert said. "The Devil's hour. Do you think anyone will stay awake that long? I have a feeling Abernathy is already asleep, if he hasn't snuck off home."

Rackem grumbled, looked hard down the Emmert Road at the restless trees and at the thick darkness at its end. He half expected someone to stroll out of it, whistling and carrying Johnathon Schmidt and Noel Oswald's severed heads in either hand. *In either clawed hand.* "We will," he said. "The parents will. Frank Oswald might. He's after his daughter, but I've known the man to be lazy."

"I'll bet Lani's awake," Talbert said. "She's been sleeping all day and gawking at the moon all night. I don't know what to do, Rackem."

The sheriff still peered down the road. He was thinking about the first night, remembering how Lani had stood on the porch and pointed at the moon, mumbling nonsense. He wondered what would become of her if Johnathon was dead. "We'll get your boy back," he said. He half believed it. "Now let's get to cover in case they do come."

"You wager they'll come from the south?" Talbert asked.

"I do."

"From the woods?"

"Yeah."

Talbert nodded. "I'll take the western side."

"I'll take the east. Keep your eyes open."

Talbert walked to the roadside and vanished within the shade below the trees. Rackem did the same. From where Talbert sat, he could see the red glow of Rackem's cigarette. Nothing more.

An hour or so passed with Talbert slouched against the tree trunk, watching for any sign of movement on the road. Occasionally, a match sparked and the scent of sulfur and smoke drifted over to him. Other than that, there was nothing of interest.

An owl hooted somewhere in the obscurity of branches to the south. Talbert did not remember ever seeing owls at the farm, but perhaps he had never noticed. He wondered what kind of owl it was. A little brown one? One of those fluffy white ones with the yellow eyes? What if it was an owl that stole Johnathon, flew away with the child and placed him in its nest alongside its eggs. What if..."

3

Talbert's eyes peeled open. He was slumped against a tree trunk, groggy and cumbersome. It was all he could do just to manipulate his droopy eyes from side to side, sweeping them across a black world without moonlight. He did not remember falling asleep. An owl had hooted. Everything had faded after that.

He tried to call for Rackem, but Talbert's voice wouldn't work. It took all his strength just to stand. And even then his body felt weighted. It was a struggle to move into the road, where a terrible darkness made it impossible to see. The trees were vague spires of black. He moved forward in a straight line until Talbert found the ditch. He went into it, fumbled blindly until he found the sheriff.

Rackem was curled in a ball, a blurry lump in a crumpled hat. Talbert turned him over. "Wake up,

Rackem." But the sheriff was fast asleep.

Talbert yanked on his beard to try and wake him. He lifted Rackem's eyelid and jabbed a finger into one of his squishy eyeballs. "Darn," he said when nothing happened, "he's out cold. This is evil at work. I know it."

Foreboding was stronger than ever as Talbert floundered out of Rackem's patch of darkness and back into the gloom of the road. A sense of doom followed him down the trail to the Henley's farm. He panted and hobbled through the dead air, feet scuffling over dirt. As Talbert came upon the house, the sensation of something evil was stronger than ever.

He did not see Mr. Ringall's body contorted awkwardly in the threshold of the Henley's stable. It was too dark. He did see the house, however, ominous in the murk with its windows flickering red and orange as if the fires of Hell raged inside.

Talbert climbed the stairs to the porch and turned the knob, allowed himself entry. Firelight played on the cedar walls of the foyer. It was the glow from the hearth; he could hear it crackle down the hall. Another sound, too. Something faint.

Cautiously, Talbert moved deeper into the home. He crept by a dark bedroom, its door open and the beds inside vacant. Five steps later and he stood in the doorway of another. There were three beds. Two were covered in heaps of tussled blankets and one contained the slumbering form of Retha Henley. Logan Reitner lay prone on the floor. Logan's hammer was out of reach and his heat blistered face held a blank, sleepy expression.

Talbert stepped into the room. "Psst, wake up. Logan, Retha, wake up. Where are the children?"

No one stirred. It was as if a poison mist had incapacitated the whole town.

"God almighty," Talbert said to himself, "please let this be a nightmare. That's all. Just a vivid nightmare."

It certainly felt like one. Talbert moved with the weighted bulk of someone submerged within a dreamscape, and things had a hushed, surreal nature to them. The way Logan Reitner lay on the floor had a pseudo quality. Retha looked like a doll, like there was no life beyond her porcelain facade.

Dream or no dream, when Talbert turned from the creepy effigies and beheld a set of shadows thrown against the wall of the corridor, the sight of them was enough to make him gasp and slap a hand over his mouth.

They originated from the parlor, two distinct shapes and one of a strange ambiguity. The two he recognized as children. He did not know which ones. They lingered patiently behind the other shadow, which was perverse in every regard.

It was hunkered on the floor with its face downturned and its back arched grotesquely. It jerked about in fast, savage motions, and its wispy hair seemed to float as it snapped its head one way and then the other, like the way a dog's head flails when it rips meat from bone. Its face was nuzzled into something it cradled beneath itself. It made loud, moist, suckling sounds.

It tilted its head back and ebony liquid dribbled off its pointed chin. Talbert shuddered. He thought he heard it laugh. The creepy shadow then raised its hand and dangled from its talons the body of a small girl, her hair brushing the floor. It tossed her aside with lazy contempt and the girl's body landed with a wet thud. The lanky shadow wiped its mouth and stood.

Standing upright, all Talbert could see of the shadow were its spindly legs; surely, he thought, distorted by the firelight. There was no way anyone could stand so tall.

It moved away from the fireplace. The children, neither beckoned nor provoked, followed behind its long, gangly legs. Their shadows stretched as shadows do, warbled and made the children's sooty aspects ugly, then vanished altogether as they entered the hallway.

Talbert listened to the monster's steps, barefoot slaps against the wooden floor panels. They neared, closer and closer and Talbert's breath caught in his throat. It was the most drawn out moment of Talbert's life. The hallway was short, yet it took a hundred hollow steps for the *thing* to reach him.

It stopped. Talbert's heart hiccupped. His stomach clenched. He could hear its raspy inhalation just outside the door, just out of sight. Talbert waited. He was torn between shutting his eyes and his desire to see the demonic shadow's true shape. He blinked, then widened his eyes and traced the fringe of the doorframe, waiting, waiting...

A grisly white face with sunken eyes and a mouthful of serrated red teeth bent from the upper corner of the doorway and smiled at Talbert.

He closed his eyes and shrieked.

4

Talbert woke, no longer screaming. It was daytime and he was sprawled in the grass on the side of the Emmert road. He tried quickly to remember the face of that awful monster, but the memory of it felt to have faded long ago. In fact, the entire ordeal seemed a distant memory from another life. By the time he sat up, Talbert had already forgotten the whole thing.

He raised a hand against the sunlight that sifted through the weave of branches above him, yawned and cracked his back. Talbert felt well rested. A full eight hours of sleep, he wagered. Then, braving the glare of light and discerning the sun's actual position in the sky, reckoned it to be much more than just eight hours. "Impossible," Talbert said. "It's got to be three in the afternoon, if not later."

Across the Emmert Road, Rackem woke in a similar daze. Talbert watched between his fingers as the sheriff bumbled about blindly in search of his hat, pulled it from a bramble of thorns and snugged it over his greasy black hair, then tilted it to block the brightness from his eyes. He too, Talbert noticed, was boggled by the presence of day. Rackem frowned and squinted upwards through the trees, grumbling quietly. The sheriff then clambered to his feet and Talbert followed suit. They met in the middle of the Emmert Road.

Rackem inspected his pocket watch. "I can't believe it," he said, tapping on the glass face. "It's half past three."

Talbert's eyes flicked to where the fireball in the sky raged above the tree line, well into its ritual descent. "Aye, it's almost dark. We've slept through the whole night and the entire day. We've missed the kidnapper. What of everyone else? Why did nobody wake us?"

"Not good," Rackem said, ignoring Talbert's questions. Dark circles hugged the sheriff's eyes and he looked old. Much older than a week past. Bits of white hair sprouted amongst the black bush of his beard. His skin sagged. Talbert thought he saw fear in Rackem's beaten face.

The sheriff buried his face in both hands and grumbled incoherently. He shook his head side to side, staggered back a few steps. When he uncovered his face, it was flushed and strained. "It can't be," he said, staring bug-eyed at Talbert. "Not here. Not in Emmert!"

"What are you talking about?" Talbert asked. It was the first time he had seen Rackem seriously distressed. It reminded him of the first time he saw his father cough.

"Our damn time," Rackem said. "It's being drained. Christ's love, we slept until nearly dusk. I can't even remember falling asleep. I doubt you can either. Yesterday we didn't wake up until almost noon. Think about tomorrow, Schmidt. Imagine waking up to darkness."

"Nonsense. How is that possible?"

"The children," Rackem said. "We need to check on them. I fear the worst."

Before Talbert could reply, Rackem was running towards the Henley's farm, one hand tucked inside his duster.

5

Logan Reitner burst through the front door just as Rackem was hurrying by the stable, Talbert rushing to catch up. The blacksmith took two short steps and puked all over the porch. He then fell to his knees, sucked in a deep breath and heaved some more.

Rackem climbed the steps two at a time. "What's going on?"

The blacksmith lifted his head, observed Rackem with wet, bright pink eyes. "Sick," he said. "It's so sick." Logan snapped his head down and spewed between his knees.

"Is he okay?" Talbert asked. But Rackem ran into the house.

Talbert lingered a moment to make sure Logan was alright. The blacksmith was slouched with his head limp and vomit on his trousers. Now he was sobbing. He sobbed harder than Talbert would have believed a man of his bulk capable, and the kind-hearted farmer had no clue how to console a blacksmith. Regretfully, Talbert turned and chased Rackem inside.

The moment Talbert entered the Henley's home, he was assaulted by a creepy sense of déjà vu. It had goosebumps crawling up his arms. The black knots in the pale cedar of the foyer created sinister faces that winked at Talbert as he passed, and the narrow hallway warbled as he entered it. The first bedroom he came to was vacant. He had somehow known it would be before he looked. He rushed to the second, anticipating something awful but not knowing what, yet there was nothing, empty beds and dusty dressers. Talbert hesitated before going into the parlor. He heard a muffled sound from the end of the hall and it made him squeamish. It reminded him of something he could not recall.

Talbert eased his way to the end of the passage and the wide threshold of the sitting room. He paused there, on the cusp of entering, and gawked without comprehension.

Everything was odd. Rackem stood inside, his boot resting on the head of a bearskin rug. He was captivated by a ragged lump of something red beside the stone fireplace, the logs charred and dead. Mr. and Mrs. Henley were in the corner of the room beside the window. Retha's face was buried in Clyde's chest and her arms were wrapped tight around him, but Clyde's attention was fixed on the same weird object that Rackem's was. Retha's dampened crying filled the room.

Puzzled but not sure why, Talbert crossed the border and into the space, past a table messy with papers and porcelain teacups, past Rackem, to the center, where a lone chair was toppled in front of the fireplace.

Talbert did not understand what was so unsettling about the lump beside the hearth. He looked at it, turned his head this way and that. It was just a pile of something, some wadded up clothes or...

Or the half-eaten corpse of a child.

No, it can't be, Talbert thought. It was unreal. The parlor was too kept. Things were in their places and everything was normal. Light washed in through the main window and made bright the space. Yet there it was. A hump of hair and meat, scrunched and small by the fireplace. And yes, the hollow of an eye socket, a row of teeth, a glint of bone swaddled in bloody rags... The half-eaten corpse of a child.

CHAPTER SEVEN

1

Talbert almost tripped over Logan Reitner as he erupted from the Henley's doorway and made for the stairs, where Logan sat on the top step with his knees drawn up and his elbows resting on them, looking deadpan across the yard. Talbert's shin collided with the blacksmith's arm and sent Talbert tumbling down the steps, but he caught himself on the railing and vaulted to the ground, then continued his brisk exit of the property.

Inside the shaded doorway of the Henley's stable, Mr. Ringall was finding his feet. He must have just woken up because he shuffled out into the sun and lifted his hand to the light, and Talbert could see the same confusion on the doctor's face that seemed a staple of that morning.

"Hey there," Mr. Ringall said. "Why'd no one wake me this morning?"

Talbert paid him no heed. He kept his head down and stormed past the stable without a word to Mr. Ringall.

The good doctor lingered in the sun and watched Talbert vanish behind some trees, scratching his head and looking dumb.

Talbert had said nothing before fleeing the Henley's house. Not to Rackem. Not to the horrified parents who quivered in the corner. Not to anyone. He had taken one hard look at the bundle of blood and bone and instantly thought of Johnathon. He had pictured his son's face pocked with teeth marks and the flesh of his tiny body half consumed, wrapped in cloth and discarded like trash. Talbert had to get home to Lani. The whole word was dying and Talbert needed to be with his wife.

He reached the Emmert Road just as Abernathy Congar was staggering out of the Mason's lane. The old fool was shabby in his dirty yellow overalls, his mangy white hair rumpled. He looked at Talbert. They locked eyes. Abernathy scratched nervously at his arm, then twisted his long legs and sprinted off in the direction of town without saying a word.

Talbert watched until Abernathy was gone, then turned south and began a steady march towards his home. He needed to return to Lani, to his wife. He needed to see with his own eyes that she still breathed. It was all that held sway in his mind, and all he could think about as sunshine slipped through breaks in the overhead foliage, tremored in his eyes and cast the world in shudders of black and bright.

He barely noticed the silence of the closing day, the absence of singing birds and in no distance the twang of a workman's tool. He kept his eyes intent on the road's horizon in anticipation of seeing his roof's sharp peak rise above the dirt, while at the same time praying to God that Lani was okay. She had to be okay.

2

In Talbert's haste to reach his house, the shape of it coming quickly into view at the end of the Emmert Road, he did not notice Pearl Tanner amble out of her gate in a tizzy and sidle up to him.

"Talbert Schmidt," she said, her voice sprightly as usual, "what a gift you are to be passing by my home at this very moment. A gift from the heavens in my time of most urgent need."

He tried to disregard her and keep walking. Talbert's house was right there, only a few more steps to the entrance. For the love of God, he could see his porch through the trees! He could see his front window gleam in the dying sunlight!

But Pearl grabbed hold of his elbow. "Please," she said, "wait just a moment. Just one moment. I beg you to hear me out."

Talbert looked into Pearl's soft brown eyes, shaded and pathetic beneath the brim of her white bonnet. He looked back to his house. Then back to Pearl. "What do you need?" he said with a sigh. "I'm in a real hurry to get home. It's an emergency."

He thought he saw a flash of victory in Pearl's face as she released his elbow and raised her palms to the sky. "Praise the Lord. Talbert Schmidt, your kindness never falters. It so happens I have an emergency of my own. A most terrible and frightening situation with my dearest husband has arose and I simply do not know what to do. Illness has come, you see, and though I try and try, I worry it is not enough. Could you please take a look at my darling? Perhaps there is something your eyes can see that mine can not."

Talbert groaned. He had no time for Pearl's foolishness. "Have you seen Doctor Ringall?" he asked. "It might be better for you to see the doctor. I have no training with medicine, I'm sorry."

"Talbert Schmidt," she said, pointing a rather stern finger at him. "Never have I known you to be a coward who turns heel when a neighbor is in need. I know your heart is as pure as polished gold, so I do. This business of mine is life or death, Talbert, and should God deem it a matter of death, then so be it. I am a servant to his will and may his judgment be done. Yet if a test of faith has been placed before us—a great trial for both you and I—then I suggest we prove our devotion, lest our sinner-born souls be damned."

Talbert sighed again. He looked at his house, still there behind the grove of trees. "I'll take a look," he said, "but I can't promise anything. You should really see

Doctor Ringall."

Pearl scowled. "I would not seek that witchdoctor or his harlot wife if my own eyes melted from their sockets and I came down with leprosy. Heathens, the pair of them. I told our kindly sheriff. I said to him, 'Sheriff, do not let these folk into Emmert. I know they may appear clean and wholesome, but the tools of their trade are forged in the fires of Hell by the Devil himself.' Alas, the sheriff chose to ignore reason. A pity, if you ask me." Pearl shook her head. "But here I stand blithering like that gossiping toad, Mrs. Ashberry. Follow me, Talbert. I will show you to my husband's room."

Talbert took one more look at his house and hung his head. Then he followed Pearl through the cobblestone path of her garden. Pearl's black and white puritan style dress reminded Talbert of the nuns in Cincinnati, at the hospital where his mother had died. He remembered following a nun through a loud and dingy corridor, patients being carted this way and that, most covered in stained sheets and everywhere people wailing. He remembered the dread that had eaten him on that walk. That same dread was with him now.

3

Talbert smelled it right away when he entered Pearl Tanner's home, the putrid scent of bile. It reeked like a butcher's shop on a hot summer day. He could taste it, too, the fumes of decaying horsemeat. The house was swarmed with blackflies.

"What is that?" Talbert asked, pinching his nose. "It reeks in here."

Pearl paused and sniffed the air, then shook her head. "I smell nothing, Talbert. Not a thing. Quickly now, my husband's room is just down the hall, next to mine."

Talbert frowned, that feeling of dread knotting his gut. He followed Pearl through her home, not finding a source of the bad odor. He looked inside a large room with brown walls and a brick fireplace that appeared unused for some time. The portrait of a young man was hung above a black dresser. An old loom collected dust in the corner.

He hurried past other rooms with dusty floors and thin white curtains, bare dressers and standing clocks. In none of the apartments did Talbert find the origin of the stench.

"The kid's rooms," Pearl said as they came upon a closed door at the end of the hall. "I rejoice in God that my boys are not here to see their beloved father in such a frail and deplorable state. I can not imagine it, Talbert, for a boy to see his father so broken. It would tarnish my husband's strong image."

"Aye." Talbert knew it well. "So it would."

"Yes, but never mind all that. Come. My husband's in here."

Pearl opened the door and stepped into what Talbert could only have described as a funeral-in-wait. It reminded him so much of Eli Schmidt's room at the end of his life that Talbert had to pause and give the place a second look. There were ornate vases on the table tops that held fresh roses and tulips, half burned candles inside brass fixtures, their wicks crispy and black. There was a pile folded laundry on the surface of an elegant vanity and a clump of blood-stained sheets on the floor beside it. Beneath the room's only window was Dennis Tanner. He appeared to be waiting for the mortician.

At first, Talbert thought Dennis was asleep. A sheet bound him tightly to a small bed and concealed Dennis from toe to chin. He looked constricted by it, like a bundled-up corpse, rigid and bloodless. All Talbert could see of the man was his face. His eyes were shut, lips tight, skin a molted gray. It took a full ten seconds for Talbert to understand that Dennis was dead. Judging by the fetid stench that seeped off his cadaver, dead for quite some time.

"Mrs. Tanner..."

"Oh, I know," she cried, rushing to Dennis' bedside and falling to her knees, looking upon him with worry. "My husband is wasting away, it is true. Just gander at my poor beloved's face. Only days ago it was handsome and vibrant, and now it is lackluster. Why, even my darling's skin is cold to the touch." As if to emphasize, Mrs. Tanner stroked Dennis' pale cheek, then looked up at Talbert. "Is there nothing you can do, Talbert? I have done all within my power and still my husband remains unwell. Can you help? Please say that you can."

Pearl blinked at Talbert with tears ready to pour from her eyes, but all Talbert could think of was madness. What sort of madness had overcome Pearl Tanner to cause her to care wholeheartedly for a rotting corpse? What about Lani? What madness tormented his wife? What demon of rage had possessed Pete Roscal and what nefarious sorcery cut short the days? What in the name of God was happening in Emmert!

"Pearl," Talbert said, swallowing nervously, "Dennis is gone."

She stared at Talbert like he was the crazy one. "No, not gone. At rest, Talbert. My husband is resting." She stood up, brushed dust off her skirt. "I understand the illness may have smitten my dear husband with a lack of vigor, but I can assure you there is life yet within."

Talbert looked him over again. Dennis' face gave the impression of having been soaked in swamp water. His eyes did not shift beneath their lids. His lips were pallid. A fly landed on the tip of his nose. Dennis did not flinch. He was dead. As dead as any man had ever been.

"You're in denial," Talbert said. "I'm sorry, but it's true. You don't need to be ashamed. You're not crazy. Lani's dug her own ditch of denial to hide in. Some people just can't accept when a loved one has--"

"Stop your foolishness," she snapped. "My husband is alive and well and is merely at rest. It is solely a byproduct of the ailment which gives the appearance of lifelessness. Nothing more."

Pearl's conviction encouraged Talbert to take a third, more critical look at Dennis, but he was still dead. A second fly landed in the nook of Dennis' left eye and began to feast on some gunk.

"My husband's lungs were the first to show signs of infection," Pearl said, using a loud, obnoxious accent and moving swiftly across the room to the vanity. "Naturally, I needed to do something. I thought the best remedy for the lungs—assuming they were clogged or dirty—was to give them a good washing."

Unease slipped into Talbert, that sudden, overwhelmingly cold fear. Pearl's back was turned to him and she fiddled with the laundry stacked on the vanity. He had a fierce desire to flee while she was occupied. Talbert could see a smudged reflection of her face in the oval mirror and swore her expression was of a maniacal nature; something of a smirk curled her lips and perhaps it was something deranged that blazed in her eyes.

Talbert gulped. "Did you say you washed Dennis' lungs? His actual lungs?"

"It was not easy." Still sorting through the laundry. "My husband has a great endurance for pain. Heaven burn me if I was not forced to retrieve a set of straps from the shed. Still, my dearest man yowled all the while. There must have been some relief, though, God provided, for sleep ensued immediately after the lungs were removed. That slumber continues still. A rest of recovery, I pray. Still, is there anything you can do to help, Talbert? If you cannot think of some way to..."

Flies descended on Dennis' face. They flew in and out of his nostrils. They buzzed inside his ears and crept along his lips. A cluster of them formed in his wilting beard and it hummed like a beehive. Talbert kept thinking there was something wrong, asides from the obvious.

Did she say straps?

Talbert looked at the bed posts. Sure enough, tied to each pole was a band of leather that wrapped down and beneath the sheet.

"Help me put them back in," Pearl was saying.

"What?" Talbert shook his head. He had missed something. "Back in?"

"Of course. How else will my husband get better if the lungs remain—Ah, here they are." Pearl held up a pair of dried-out lungs. She had washed the red, meaty things with the rest of the laundry. "You can assist me," she went on. "It was difficult for me to get them out, and I fear I may have more trouble putting them back in."

Talbert stuttered. He had no idea what to say. He stepped backward with his mouth opening and closing, until his legs banged against a dresser and a flower vase fell to the ground and smashed. The shatter made him jump, but Pearl hardly noticed. She stalked towards him with the lungs outstretched and an innocent look on her face. She stopped at Dennis' bedside, placed the fat organ gently on an uncluttered dresser, then went to work pulling free the sheet that bound Dennis to the bed.

With the sheet loose, she paused and looked at Talbert. "Come closer. Let me show you where they go."

Pearl pulled the sheet down to Dennis' waist, revealing his soggy, mutilated torso. A raw cavity dominated his chest, the edges of it soft and mangled from where a dull blade had struggled through flesh and meat. Organs that were once red and healthy were now black and yellow and festering. His ribcage was splintered as if a living creature and hatched and then broken out of his chest.

"I admit," Pearl said, "my handiwork is not my greatest attribute. My hands are more adapted to linen and weaving than the workings of the human anatomy."

Talbert gawked. Hundreds of blackflies droned in protest at the uncovering of their nest. They poured out of

Dennis in a relentless black cloud and flew around him in angry spirals. Within their gory hollow, all was yellow with blight and pools of maggots writhed.

"You've gone mad," Talbert said, unable to compose himself any longer. "This whole town has gone goofy and you along with it. Look at your husband, Pearl. For the love of God, you've mutilated him"

"Control yourself," Pearl said sharply, not looking away from Dennis' fly infested corpse. "I would prefer it if my husband stays asleep while we insert the lungs. These blasted flies make enough noise."

"No," Talbert said, almost a whisper. "No, this is wrong. You've gone too far. I'm going to get Rackem and tell him what you've done."

She eyed Talbert suspiciously. "Are you quite well? Perhaps you have an affliction of your own."

"You're crazy." Talbert was bewildered. "A lunatic. It's you who's afflicted, Mrs. Tanner. There's something wrong inside your head. You're sick, you hear me. Sick!"

"Yes," she said, her terrible madness shining outwards. "I see it now. There is a sickness in your head. I believe it would be a good idea for us to wash your brain, Talbert. I can take it out for you, give it a good scrubbing. You will be as good as new after that. No more yelling."

Talbert had enough. He was horrified by her leisure insanity and tried to flee through the open doorway.

But Pearl was fast. She intercepted him, knife brandished in her hand, the tip of it pointed at his face. Whether she had pulled it from somewhere beneath her dress, Talbert had no idea, but it shook in her grip as she threatened him.

"Not another step," Pearl said, "for as God is my witness, I will carve that brain from your skull before I allow you to spread your filthy disease through Emmert."

Fear moved Talbert's feet. He didn't feel like getting scalped. Talbert made a break for the door and

Pearl lunged at him with a shriek of insanity. The knife in her hand sought to slice off Talbert's nose, but missed as he jerked back and slammed into the wall.

It became a fight for survival. Pearl was eager to cut into him. He had to hold her wrists back with both hands to keep the tip of her knife from penetrating his eyeball. Still, the blade cut small slits across the bridge of Talbert's nose as it wavered left and right.

She was too strong. Stronger than she should have been. Pearl's skinny arms overpowered Talbert and with one crazed shove and a grunt, she broke his guard and the knife sailed along the side of his head.

"Gaah," Talbert cried. He made a fist and swung it upwards, connected with Pearl's jaw. She stumbled. He pushed away from the wall and, fueled by adrenaline, punched her square in the face. The force of it swept Pearl off her feet and she cracked her skull off the corner of a dresser on her way down. She crumpled up against Dennis' bedframe and fell dormant, thin trickles of red weeping down her forehead.

Talbert stood panting. His chest heaved and his fists remained clenched. He had never hit someone before. It felt wrong. His knuckles hurt. Also, his ear throbbed. He thought for sure it had been cut off. Carefully, Talbert stepped over Pearl's outstretched legs and looked in the vanity mirror.

The side of Talbert's head was wet with blood and more of it oozed from a gash stretching from the corner of his eye past his ear. The ear itself was cut in half. "Damn you," he said, twitching and mad. "Damn this whole cursed town!"

Talbert looked one last time upon the gruesomeness, the hollowed-out pit in Dennis' chest and the restless blackflies that swarmed around it. Pearl appeared to be dead. Her white bonnet dangled around her neck by its drawstrings and her entire face was streaked with blood.

"Madness," Talbert said, "utter madness."

CHAPTER EIGHT

1

Crimson bloomed in the western sky, painting the gathered pilgrims ominous shades of red and pink. More than two thirds of Emmert's population were gathered before Emmert's gates. There was Carlos O' Brian, his wife and their brood of five younglings. There were the Masons and their two nervous sons. Abernathy Congar lingered near the front of the group with a wooden pipe clenched between his teeth and smoke drifting past his wicker hat. His Scythe was where he had left it, forgotten in a cluster of tomato plants in the Mason's front yard. Logan Reitner and his pregnant wife sat silently on horseback. Upon hearing of the maimed girl, Beatrice Reitner did not care if riding a horse while six months pregnant was dangerous or not; she just wanted to leave. It was much the same for everyone in attendance. They were all willing to abandon their belongings and vacate Emmert once news of murder and mutilation had reached their ears.

      That news alone would not have been enough to convince most of them. It was the unavoidable fact that daylight shone less and less each frigid day in a season that should have boasted longer hours and warmer temperatures. That was what pushed them to flee in the chill of night, lest they wake up to find their children dead and a perpetual darkness outside their windows. The word on everyone's lips was *witchcraft*.

      While the mass of citizens stood anxiously awaiting

the last migrants to join their ranks so they could move on to Fort Boise, all anyone could talk about was witchcraft. It was a simple explanation for simple folk. In their world of superstition and paranoia, witchcraft made perfect sense. What other reason could there have been for their misfortune, if not that a witch was sent by the Devil to corrupt their Godly ways?

Abernathy Congar had been the first to bang on doors and spread the warning of a wicked one in Emmert, and he perpetuated that rumor throughout the brief day. "A pile of the winged rodents," he had said to Davis Somer and his wife, Martha, as he stood on their stoop and spoke loud enough for both neighbors to hear. "Right there in the Mason's hearth. I saw the burnt buggers with my own eyes. Only a witch could have done such evil. A mistress of Satan, I tell you. She must have dumped—oh, I reckon fifty crows—down the Mason's chimney. They were already dead when they got all jammed up amongst the logs and the ash. Only the ones on the bottom burnt. They were all black and crispy and their wings were singed, but the ones on top were untouched by any flame. They were just dead, clogged up in the flume God knows how high."

It was enough to incite panic, a panic that escalated into wild hysteria when Frank Oswald began telling the same story and Logan Reitner came forward with the news of the butchered girl and the two that were missing. Within hours every parent was bundled up next to their children in front of Emmert's main gates in anticipation of a cold night on the road. Only the few without kids remained home. The old or the skeptical. Mrs. Ashberry watched the congregation from her porch. Pastor Marble was nowhere to be found. Miss Huntly cowered behind her window and peered through the blinds. She knew all too well the accusations that would be thrown around regarding the identity of the witch. As Emmert's only single female, she was an easy target. Larissa Huntly was too beautiful not to be named Bride of Satan by the God-fearing hags of Emmert.

"We can't just leave everything behind," June O'Brian said to her father. "What will we do in Fort Boise, Daddy? I've never left Emmert. What if someone steals everything from the shop? What if there are wolves or Indians?"

"Oh hush," he said. "Most of the valuables are strapped to the cart. There are no wolves going to eat fifty people. We can come back for our things later. Unless you want to get cooked up by a witch, I suggest we leave with everyone else right now."

Carlos looked above the throng of anxious people toward the western sky. The red flare of moments ago was already beginning to fade and much of the clouds had blackened to blend with the bruised atmosphere as it transitioned from pink to stark jet. "I'd like to get out of here soon," he said, "before night falls."

"The witch can't touch us," June said, "not with so many people here."

Carlos gave his daughter a sharp look. "If everyone falls asleep at the snap of her fingers, she can do whatever the heck she wants. You best believe that."

June's face went red. She inspected the shabby farmers and tradesmen standing with their kin and their carts, horses and donkeys. "Why don't we just tie her up and kill her? Better her than us."

"June," Her mother said, harshly. "What's gotten into you?"

"Leave her alone," Carlos said. "The girl's right. I only wish I knew who it was. I'd string her up myself."

"Probably that Huntly woman," Patty Mason whispered, leaning in to join the conversation. "I hear she hasn't had a man since her husband passed. I also hear she poisoned him. Some kind of Pagan ritual. Thomas Weathers apparently saw a hooded woman lurking around the Oswald's place the night their daughter was taken. I heard the woman's coat was identical to one Miss Huntly owns. I doubt it's a coincidence."

"Nonsense," Carlos said. "I've known Larissa a long time and I knew her husband, too. She's a lonely widow. If we're going to start pointing fingers, my dollar's on Emily Roscal. I'm starting to wonder if she didn't push her own kid down that well. Maybe Angela saw too much. Maybe she killed Pete, too, and that's why he's not here."

Patty considered, then tugged on Darrel's sleeve. "Who do you think the witch is? Little June O' Brian has the right of it. We'd be better off finding the cursed harlot so we can put an end to this nightmare, rather than sneaking off into the night."

Darrel snarled at his wife, then glared at Carlos, June, his own two boys, and half a dozen other folk who were listening.

"I don't think Emily Roscal or Miss. Huntly have the physical prowess to dump a hundred dead crows down my chimney, nor the supernatural power to lull a whole town to sleep. You people are apt to start a blood-thirsty riot. You're soon to get someone killed." He fixed a rueful glare on Patty. "Keep your mouth shut about lynchings."

"No one is getting lynched," Logan Reitner said from atop his horse. His voice boomed over the others and made them seem small. "We don't know if there is a witch. No one has any clue what's happening. You're all just scared, and rightfully so. I am too. The only thing we know for sure is that our children are in grave danger, and that's enough to kick my butt out of town. Maybe if we remove the children for a while, that danger will leave and we can return home. There are no thieves in Emmert to loot your things. Asides from a few weak crops, all will be well in time. Now can someone open that darn gate so we can leave before night sweeps us under its rug?"

"Where's Thomas?" someone shouted, and again

a rabble rose in the air.

2

Rackem heard the commotion from the dank confines of his cellar, where he sat on his usual perch with his back against the wall and his eyes open wide to the darkness. He grunted as he stood, unsteady on legs that felt to have no bones. Rackem had to catch himself against the wall and he almost dropped the bottle of whiskey in his hand. It clattered against the stone.

Sobriety had not lasted long for Sheriff Rackem. The instant he had returned home from the massacre at the Henley's farmhouse he had opened his liquor cabinet and begun guzzling booze like a man parched from years of thirst. It was the horror of the girl's corpse that had made him lose control. That and the terrible truth of what had been unleashed in Emmert.

Rackem threw open the front door so hard it clattered against the outside wall and drew the attention of every man assembled. Darrel Mason and his son, Samwell, were in the middle of dragging apart the huge wooden doors of the front gate, and paused to regard the drunk sheriff as he ambled clumsily down his steps.

"Stop," Rackem said, holding up his hands and unwittingly displaying his liquor bottle for the whole town to see. "Where are you going? It's not safe out there."

Rackem looked up to see Logan Reitner sitting on his horse in a deerskin jerkin and a beaver fur hat. "Logan, where are you going?" Rackem reached up as if to grab Logan's foot and pull him from his horse, but he tripped and fell sideways, his bottle twirling through the air and his face landing in the dirt.

Groaning, Rackem lifted himself up. The first thing he spotted was his bottle, upside down and draining into the dirt. He went to it—scuttled across the ground like he had no legs and uprighted his whiskey, then slurped the spilled booze from a muddy puddle.

"Pathetic," Patty Mason said. She stood above the

sheriff, looking like she wanted to spit in his hair.

Rackem had left his duster somewhere on the floor of his house. His hat, too. All he wore were dark boots and dark trousers, a tattered white tunic stained with too many nights of vomit. He looked more like a drunk peasant than a town sheriff.

"Look at yourself," Patty said. "Two sheets to the wind and a shameful mess to boot. How do you reckon to protect us in the state you're in? No, I don't think you can. Me and mine will take our chances on the road. We're off to seek help from the men in Fort Boise. Your ambush didn't work."

Rackem lifted his head and a brown mixture of whiskey and dirt dribbled off his lips. "Patty..." But she was already gone, absorbed into the huddle. No one else would meet Rackem's miserable stare.

"Let's go," Darrel said from the front line. "No time to waste. Night's upon us."

The convoy creaked and groaned and trudged forward, while Rackem lay stunned and too far-gone in booze to do anything but gape at them and beg. "Abernathy, don't leave me." But the old timer nodded his straw hat to the sheriff and kept on.

Mrs. Somer stooped down to Rackem as she passed. "Clean yourself up," she said, then left him with his hands outstretched like a worthless beggar and followed the others out the gates.

3

He was alone. Rackem sat on the bottom step of his porch and drank, let the harsh stuff pour down his throat. He winced, wiped his mouth, and stared across the street at Mrs. Ashberry's house. The plump lady was bent over her railing, chubby cheeks puffed in a mirthful grin. "What?" Rackem said.

Mrs. Ashberry laughed. "It would seem you are the sheriff of a ghost town. Good luck tending to them."

She waved and went inside.

Out of the newly fallen black appeared Miss. Huntly. She came leisurely down the road in bright colors that seemed in contradiction of the night, and stopped below where Rackem sat drinking on the steps of his porch.

"They'll be back," she said. "You'll see. Everyone will return when they remember how disastrous and uncomfortable the road travelled is. A walking nightmare, as I remember. They're just scared, that's all. Frank and Abernathy did a splendid job stirring them into a panic and convincing them the sun won't be shining here tomorrow." Miss. Huntly looked up at the sky, shook her head. "Silly men. Of course the sun will shine. The light of the sun is the light of God and can never cease to shine."

Rackem grumbled and took a swig from his bottle. He eyed the beautiful woman, vivid against the darkness in luxuriant wrappings of red, her ringlets of gold. He had to squint to see her properly, otherwise one became two and he felt like vomiting. "They might," Rackem said. "They might not."

"They will. Trust me. Those people love Emmert too much to forsake it. They love you, too. They're just scared." She shifted awkwardly. "Can I sit with you a minute, sheriff? I don't want to be a burden. You know I couldn't stand to be a pest. But if it's all the same to you, I would like to sit for a minute."

Although Miss Huntly's face was a blur from where he sat, Rackem could hear her smile. The woman's voice was a sweet melody in his ears. It always was. It soothed him, and he scooched over to make room without grumbling once. "Are you cold?" she asked. "You're in nothing but a flimsy old shirt and breeches."

"I'm fine."

"Yes, I suppose you are. All that whiskey must be good for something."

"Good for all kinds of things." Rackem took a long

drink as if to prove it.

Larissa sighed and placed a hand on Rackem's knee. "You did your best. I know you did. No one else could have done a better job at finding those kids, even if you didn't find them in the end. Some things are just bigger than one man. Even you. Still, you are a good man. A good sheriff, too."

"In the end?" Rackem jerked his leg, knocking Larissa's hand off it. "What end? It's not over yet. Not by a mile. I won't stop until I've found all four of the missing children, or at least discovered their fates."

She smiled and this time he did see it. "Of course you will. You are such a hero."

Rackem grumbled and turned his bottle upside down, drained the last few drops. "I need more. I'm going inside."

"May I?" she asked.

"No."

Rackem tried to get up, but his legs were useless and he sat right back down. "Shit!" He threw his empty bottle into the street.

"Here." Larissa wrapped her arm around the grubby man and he could feel the weight of her breasts against his shoulder. He tried to wriggle free but she scolded him. "Quit it. let me help you."

Reluctantly, Rackem obeyed. Larissa lifted him to his feet. He was unsteady and she had to wrap another hand around his stomach to keep him from slipping backwards. The tips of her fingers felt like talons trying to break his skin. "One foot at a time," she said, and guided him slowly into the house.

Inside was somehow darker than out. It certainly smelt worse. The tangy aroma of urine and poison hung in the air as Larissa hoisted Rackem into the depths of his foyer. He tried nudging her in the direction of his liquor cabinet. Drunk as a beggar and blind as a bat, he could still navigate his house with ease.

Larissa bumped into the cabinet and a dozen whiskey bottles clinked like toxic wind chimes. "Don't even think about it," she said. "I'm taking you straight to bed." She yanked Rackem away from the whiskey and he gave a meager protest. He groaned and half-heartedly dug his feet into the floor like a stubborn child, but ultimately let her take him.

She dumped Rackem in his bed. He lay there, stone-drunk while Larissa loitered uninvited his dark room. She found a matchbox on his bedside table and lit one, used it to light one of the lanterns that hung off the rafters. Then Miss. Huntly began to nose about Rackem's room.

The sheriff sat up in bed. He looked around, dazed, as if he had just woken up. He spotted his duster crumpled on the floor and used his foot to drag it to him, then searched through the pockets for his pouch of tobacco. Rackem tossed his duster back on the floor and began to roll a cigarette. He crafted a much better smoke drunk than he did sober.

"Nothing to see," he said to Larissa as she nosed around. "Just dust and old trinkets. Nothing that would interest a woman like you."

"A woman like me?" She scoffed. "I'll be the judge of what interests a woman like me."

Rackem snickered and blew smoke out his nose. He relaxed as best he could while watching Larissa snoop about his place. She was more beautiful than normal in the lamplight. Every small imperfection of her skin was erased by shadow. Miss. Huntly looked polished and perfect, the way she must have looked at sixteen. Rackem thought she could have passed for a rich duchess in her red fox fur coat. He wondered what on Earth had kept Larissa in Emmert after Yohan Huntly had passed on.

"What's this?" she asked, kneeling in front of Rackem's strongbox.

Rackem grumbled to himself. He had never told anyone about the box. Even he had forgotten about it for years beneath all that whiskey. Until a few nights ago when he had gone out in the woods behind Talbert's house. Talbert hadn't lived there back when Rackem buried it, twenty damn years ago.

"Grab me a drink," Rackem said. He was so drunk. He didn't care. Emmert was in flames. What was the harm in telling a story? "Get me a drink and I'll tell you what's in the box."

4

He was smoking another cigarette by the time Larissa returned. He looked sullen. In the pale glow of the lamp, Rackem's yellow-tinged skin was set in deep wrinkles and his droopy eyes reflected an ocean of sadness. He looked elderly, a worn-out veteran perched on the edge of his deathbed as he thought back on a life of defeat, like he was alone in the world and regretted not dying sooner.

Larissa placed the glass of whiskey in Rackem's hand. He would not meet her eyes. "Sit," he said, voice raspy and tarnished by drink. "Here, beside me."

She did. She cupped her hands in her lap and looked intently at the sheriff, who stared dully at the strongbox as he began his tale.

"I was not born an old man. I was young once. Many years before Emmert, many years before I built this house, I was a young man. I was born in New York City. My father worked the docks. He made scraps and in turn I was fed with scraps. I left when I was old enough to hate him. I haven't seen him since."

Rackem sighed and took a drag off his smoke. "I never had any friends as a kid. Never saw the point. I spent my youth rambling from town to town, not looking for anything and not wanting any of it. I entered the fur trade to earn whiskey money. We were tracking a score of beaver hides that were stolen by Indians near to the

Hudson River when I got lost. I was just a kid. I didn't know any better. They put a rifle in my hands and I shot a handful of the redskins down myself. I didn't know.

"The others in my company left without me. I don't blame them, though I did for a long time. In those woods it was dim and damp and every night I slept wet and shivering, afraid of the dark. I had heard the fur traders tell stories of beasts and spooks that ate men who got lost out there. I didn't believe them until I was alone in the woods. The sounds of the forest at night can stir up all kinds of imaginings to a lone man, none of them pleasant. Something about the solitude, I reckon.

"It was during day that I saw the real beast. It mauled me with paws bigger than my head and left me torn in more spots than you'd believe. I lay bleeding in the soil and I watched the bear saunter off on all fours like nothing had happened. I didn't fight it. I didn't much care. I had some tobacco left and I crawled to a tree trunk. I figured it looked good for dying. I sat against it and smoked, not much of a thought in my head in the way of life. My existence until then had been hard and loveless. I didn't care.

"I woke sometime later swaddled in deerskins, feverish and sick. Some hunters of the Northern Paiute had found my worthless body and dragged me back to their camp. I don't know why. It was them who had stolen the furs and me who had shot at least four of them dead. Still, they brought me back. I awoke in the shaman's hut, the things in it strange and barbaric. Skin rugs covered the earthen floor and antlers were hung from strings, odd trinkets fashioned of bone that shined red in the firelight. The old healer sealed my wounds and forced me to swallow some rank tonics, then allowed me rest. It took months before I was well enough to leave, and it was in that time that I met her."

Larissa was on the edge of Rackem's bed, lost in his story. "Who?" she asked.

Rackem kept on like he didn't hear her. "She was as young as I was, but beautiful beyond her years. She had a majestic grace that I had never witnessed during all my wanderings, and a gentle nature that I have yet to capture in another woman. Her skin was mahogany, her hair silky black. It was like God had carved her from the most precious redwood and gave her features too delicate and too fascinating to bestow upon more than one soul, her soul itself a fragment of Heaven. Anyway, we fled together once I was healed. I don't know how either of us knew it would happen. We just did. Our eyes spoke without words."

Rackem sighed and swallowed the last drops of whiskey from his glass, then placed it on his bedside table.

"During my time with the Paiute Indians, I learned many things. Their traditions were primal to me, and I saw them as wild savages, base and filthy. When they clustered around their bonfires at night, wearing beige loincloths and their faces painted like demons, and danced and howled and banged their shabby drums, I envisioned the world before God's light, when men had no reprieve from sin and lived squalid as naked apes, gathered around petty fires to shield themselves from the dark horrors of the night.

"Well, they still believed in dark horrors. They believed as strong as I believe in God that evil spirits lurked beyond the glow of their pyres. Understandable, seeing as they were never graced by the love of God. One such monster struck more fear in their hearts than any other. More than Owl Women or Skinwalkers. More than the little cannibals known as the Teihiihan, or the spirits of the dead. They called this monster Skudakumooch. They were terrified of it.

"Skudakumooch was once a female shaman who practiced forbidden witchcraft and who's body rose after death, gross and malformed. Its soul was forever tainted by the black arts it toyed with during life and as a result, she, Skudakumooch, became compelled to harvest and consume the organs of children, and to torment the adults of whichever unfortunate encampment she decided to stalk. She could change her form, from woman to monster, and she could lull entire towns to sleep, steal the daylight straight from the sky with her magic. From what I understood, Skudakumooch refused to leave until every child had been taken back to her nest and eaten. The Paiute were horrified of it. Any time a youngster went missing or someone began to act strange, we were forced to pack up and move, and I hobbled behind them. I never believed their ridiculous myths. I never believed in witches. I never believed in Skudakumooch. I never..."

The booze had caught up with Rackem. He hiccupped. His eyes crossed and his head sagged, drooping to his chest.

"Sheriff," Larissa said, "are you alright?"

Rackem grumbled and tipped over. He was snoring before his head hit the mattress.

"No," Larissa said. "Your story. Sheriff, you must finish your story. Do you think it's the Skoodamoo who's tormenting Emmert? What's in the box? Don't leave me without answers." She tried to shake him awake, pleaded and pinched his leg and kicked at his foot. It was no good. Rackem snored like an ox and Larissa was left disappointed and sour, the man's unexpected story not half told.

She left Rackem's house feeling ripped off. Miss. Huntly had never known anything about Rackem's past until tonight, and just when he had begun to weave an interesting picture of an adventurous youth, the drunk bastard fell asleep.

Standing now on his porch, shivering though she was bundled tightly in her fox coat. It was an eerie night in Emmert. Not a single light blazed in any window, and not a thread of smoke rose from any chimney. It was cold too, and Larissa could see her breath. She descended Rackem's porch and each click of her heel was a wooden ping that resonated into the depths of that still void. She reached the road and walked slowly towards her house.

Miss. Huntly felt hungry eyes leering at her before she got more than ten paces. She stopped, the scuffle of her feet stifled and the silence come like a crashing wave. She looked around, at the blank space under Rackem's porch, at the spiked pillars of Emmert's wall, at the bony trees behind Mrs. Ashberry's house. Everywhere was shadow. Nothing moved. Still, dread crept down her spine and she hurried along.

"Silly woman," Larissa whispered. "There are no Skoomachoos. The sheriff's a crazy drunk."

Just then a yowl pierced the stillness and made Larissa's blood run cold. Had someone just screamed for help? She twirled to look behind her. There was nothing, no one. Mrs. Ashberry's residence was a vague hut in the distilled moonlight and Rackem's house was totally shrouded by darkness. She listened for a second scream, but none came. Blood pumping, Larissa jogged the short distance to her house. Once inside, she lit a fire in the hearth and took shelter in its flickering light. She fell asleep on the floor. In Larissa's dreams, she was tormented by a monstrous witch with dead gray skin and sunken eyes.

5

Emily Roscal did not find it curious when she awoke halfway through the day. When she did finally amble out of her bedroom after an hour of staring at the ceiling and contemplating how difficult it would be to craft a noose, Emily wandered sluggishly into the kitchen and looked out the window. She never noticed the sun lingering far below its zenith, the pastel colors bright on the horizon. All Emily noticed was the well—a giant tombstone in the center of her yard—and the grove of apple trees to the south where Angela's grave remained empty. Hopefully Pete would be back soon to rebury Angela. Maybe after that, Emily Roscal would hang herself in the stable.

She couldn't eat. Emily filled a glass with warm water and went onto the porch, sat in her wicker chair and stared forlornly at the well, her mind in ruin. Why had she done that? Her baby, Angela... Why?

Emily stayed like this until the sun set and a cruel chill settled in the air. She went inside to put on some warmer clothes, then went back onto the veranda in a thick blouse, a wool blanket draped over her shoulders. The yard was dark. It looked haunted. The grove of apple trees to the south was spooky and their limbs were skeletal and black. The docile sheep in their pen were vague clumps of shadow and the well looked like a narrow cavemouth rearing out of the ground. Emily's eyes fell on Pete's work shed and she shuddered. Emily hated that squat building. She hated its red tile roof and the crude iron flume jutting out the top. She hated the loud saw noises that reverberated out of its walls and ruined her peaceful afternoons. There was no sound now, of course. Pete was gone. Emily suspected he was not coming back.

Something about the shed caught Emily's eye. She stood, letting the blanket fall from her shoulders and crumple on the deck. She shuffled to the banister and squinted down at the shed. The bulky lock that Pete had obtained from Carlos O' Brian had been left unsecured. There was nothing to bar her from opening the door. "Some surprise," she muttered, and went to investigate.

The lock was indeed unfastened. The metal U dangled from its fixture and just outside of the lock's casing. Emily removed it and threw it in the grass. Taking a deep breath, she pushed open the door.

It was dark and she had no lantern. There were no windows inside the shed. Emily relied on the rapidly fleeting daylight to guide her. At first, Emily did not understand. She had expected some marvelous contraption, but all she could see were metal bars and things hung from high hooks. It was too dark. She stood in the threshold a moment and allowed her eyes to adjust, then furrowed her brows in confusion. There were dozens of homemade cages suspended from trusses that looked like birdcages—like the showroom of a pet store, and small, obscure lumps filled them all. "Birds? Are those dead birds?"

There was something else too, on the floor in the very back where the shadows cloaked everything. It moved.

Emily stepped back, startled. "Hello?" She said, hoping it was a racoon or even just a rattlesnake hidden amongst the dimly lit clutter of tools and tin in the back.

No one responded and the shadows did not shift again, but Emily knew something was back there. She fumbled on the walls for a lantern, found one and used it as a beacon of light, orange radiance revealing the dozens of birdcages suspended from the rafters, their bars warped by Pete's shoddy craftsmanship. The rear of the shed was still vague; the lantern's light could not penetrate the layers of gloom. Emily had to sneak closer, arm and lamp outstretched, eyes intent on the thinning blackness, outlines being revealed, short boxes becoming clear, the light flooding in a sudden torrent over something that looked like a dog kennel, two rows of makeshift cages, and there, moving frantically behind the rusted bars...

"Lord in Heaven." Emily gasped. She staggered backwards and the darkness swarmed in to reclaim what she had seen.

"What is it, darling?"

Emily shrieked and spun around, flailing the lantern and almost smashing it over Pete's head. Her husband stood below her, short and stocky outside the doorframe.

"I thought I told you it was a surprise?" he said,

flashing black, gunk filled teeth in a sinister grin. His whole body was coated in sludge. He looked like a swamp dweller, someone who basked in mud and rolled through the dirt. Not one inch of him was clean.

"What have you done?" Emily said, slapping Pete across the face. "How could you?" Another slap. "You're a monster. A horrible monster."

She tried to hit him again but Pete caught her wrist. "I told you to wait," he said. Then Pete cackled and spoke in his inhuman accent, twisted in nefarious hilarity. "It's not ready yet, fret, fret, fret. I need another, not your older brother. Yes, yes, one more, maybe a little whore" He threw his head to the sky and laughed.

"You're not my husband," Emily said, tearing her hand from Pete's grasp and stumbling backwards, closer to the rear of the shed. "I don't know who you are, but you're not Pete. Pete would never—could never have done this." She spat the words at him, Pete licking his mud crusted lips and pursuing her deeper into the shed. "You're a lunatic in Pete's clothes. You're the Devil. That's right, the Devil. The Devil has possessed my husband!"

The light from Emily's lantern flickered at Pete's encroaching presence, balked before him so that Pete was as black as the muck that laminated him. He smiled, moved towards Emily as she backed deeper into the shadows at the rear of the shed. "Stay away," she said, bird cages stuffed with dead crows clanking against her shoulders. "I mean it, no closer. I'll scream. God help me I'll scream."

Pete opened his mouth and made a strange sound with his throat, black slime dripping from his upper pallet to his tongue.

Emily screamed.

"Help! Help me! The Devil is in my husband! Please, he's going to--"

The glass lantern shattered and all went dark.

CHAPTER NINE

1

Banging on the shed door, screaming all damn night. Talbert was sick of it. His wife's mind was shattered and Talbert couldn't fix it. He had gone out there and listened to Lani's demented rambling. "They riot in their cages," she had said, staring at the shed doors. "The Devil's within. The Devil's within!"

Talbert had left Lani to her mania. He couldn't deal with it. Half his ear was cut off and he was covered in blood, the deranged Mrs. Tanner laying dead on the floor and Dennis' body a fly-infested shell. It was a miracle that Talbert fell asleep at all. He was thinking about Johnathon, about Noel and the Henley's kidnapped sons. They were alive somewhere. Talbert knew it. Some godless bastard had his boy and the other kids locked up some place. Talbert was beginning to suspect it was someone in Emmert. The townsfolk had all gone crazy. Evil had slithered into their peaceful, God-loving town and spread its corruption. Talbert had seen the dementia in Pearl's eyes. He had seen it in Lani's face every night since Johnathon's vanishing. He had seen the unnatural rage in Pete Roscal. And little Angela... Talbert suspected she had not simply fallen into that well.

Too much. All of it. Talbert had killed Pearl and his son was the victim of a monster, people's children being massacred and the whole town gone to hell. Talbert wondered if there would be daylight on the morrow, or if

God's light truly had been revoked and he would wake to a horrible darkness. He was worried about Lani sneaking into the room while he slept and carving out his lungs. He was thinking about it he heard the scream. He thought someone was shouting for help. And that was when Talbert fell asleep.

Now it was daytime and Lani was at rest in their bed. Talbert was on his horse, strutting slowly down the Emmert Road. He did not understand why it was so quiet. Wind whistled through the trees and flowers that should have been in bloom were wilting on branches, dead leaves being swept down the road. It was cold. There was not a soul around. Laying in the dust outside the Somer's gate was a teddy bear, trampled by hooves and its button eye dangling by a thread.

It felt like Armageddon. The red sky made Talbert feel like judgement day had come, already started in the west and was soon to roll over the land in a storm of fire and brimstone. He could already see the kiln in the clouds raging.

When he reached the end of town, Talbert knew something had happened. Outside Rackem's house was a mess of footprints and hoofprints, wagon tracks and horse shit. Emmert's gate was wide open. There had obviously been a mass exodus while Talbert was at home, bandaging up his ear and washing blood off him. Why had no one told him?

Talbert knocked on Rackem's door. Surely the sheriff had not abandoned hope and rode away in the night. But the sheriff did not answer his door. Talbert banged, jiggled the knob, shouted at the window, "Open up, Rackem. Where's everyone gone? Where's my boy?"

Inside the house, hunkered in the sweaty darkness of his room, Sheriff Rackem clutched his precious box to his bare chest, patches of black hair like an old dog stricken by disease. He looked mad, a rotted goblin with stringy black hair and yellow eyes in the gloom of his shack, clinging to an ill-gotten treasure. The whole place reeked like booze, like vomit. Rackem opened the box and looked inside. "There are no more children," he said. "They've all gone. They're safe. There's nothing more for her to take."

He nodded, listening to the bones. "You're right," he said. "I must protect the town. If the people return to Emmert with their children and the witch is still here..."

Another whisper from the box of bones.

"Yes," Rackem said, "I know what I must do."

He shut the lid to the box and locked it. Rackem sat back on the floor, took a drink of whiskey and listened to Talbert Schmidt bang on his door. Poor Talbert. Rackem couldn't face him. It was Rackem's fault the Schmidt boy was gone. He had ventured into the woods and dug up his bone box. Why? Because Rackem was a sad old drunk. He had wanted to see their remains one last time. How could Rackem have known the witch would smell the afterburn of her own evil?

2

Talbert sat on the steps of Rackem's porch. The bastard wasn't home. Talbert feared Rackem and the rest of Emmert had absconded in the night. Now Talbert was alone, his boy and three other children held captive somewhere in the town. He had to find them. But where to start? A devil's sunset already bruised the sky. Soon would come the night.

Talbert pinched his nose. "Where are you, Johnathon? Lord, please give me a sign."

As if in answer, a door creaked open down the street, the sound of it unwinding loudly in the stillness. Larissa Huntly poked her head out and looked cautiously into the road, still in fear of being lynched. But she saw Talbert and smiled, gave him a wave and hurried over to meet him. Was Miss. Huntly Talbert's sign from God?

She looked worse than he had ever seen her. "I

wish I could say lovely morning," Miss. Huntly said from the bottom of Rackem's porch, "but it is not a lovely morning. Not lovely at all." She had heavy bags under her eyes, a bland yellow dress on. "Is the sheriff awake? He was in rough shape last night, poor man."

"There's no answer," Talbert said. "I fear him and the rest of Emmert ran away in the night. Only God knows where they went."

"Not the sheriff," Larissa said. "He stayed. The rest of them left, Mr. Schmidt. Just about the whole town took to the road for Fort Boise. Everyone's scared of the witch. Frank and Abernathy did a swell job of putting the fear of God in our townsfolk. There was a lot of talk last night about children being murdered and kidnapped, about eternal night descending on Emmert. Anyone with love for the kin left town. I'm afraid only a few people remain."

Talbert wasn't surprised. The people of Emmert were a superstitious lot, wary of Indians and scared of demonic creatures who lived in the woods. They feared God's wrath. Of course they had run away at the first sign of a witch. Talbert was more surprised no one had dragged Larissa from her house and burned her at the stake.

"Can't blame them," he said. "God's revoked the sun, his very light. Their children are being slain and an apocalypse blooms on the horizon. Were it not for Johnathon and Lani, I reckon I'd be following behind them."

Larissa climbed up the stairs. "Yes, Mr. Schmidt, perhaps I should have joined them too. Yet I can not leave my home, the home Yohan built for us. Emmert is mine as it is yours. I will stay to the end. Besides, someone must look after our sheriff. I bet he's sleeping off a hangover right now. He was quite drunk last night and acting very strange."

Oh no, Talbert thought, *not Rackem too.* "Strange

how?"

"He was disturbed," Larissa said. "There is a creepy box in his room, and when I asked what was in it, the sheriff told me a story about a witch. He called it a..." Larissa screwed up her face. "A skakacho? Anyway, the sheriff told me about an Indian woman he had loved... but then he fell asleep."

"A skooka-what?" Talbert asked.

Larissa shrugged. "A skakacho. He said it harvests the organs of children, steals them and torments all the people in a town. He said it was an Indian legend, that all the Injuns were scared of it."

Talbert blinked at the woman, sighed and buried his face in his hands. He was in over his head. skakatoos? Indian legends? Witches in the woods? Talbert was a godly man. He knew only of the bible and of the eternal damnation of sinners. Talbert was ill-equipped to deal with monsters. He needed Rackem's help to get his son back. It seemed the sheriff knew more than he had let on.

Talbert got up and hammered on Rackem's door. "Sheriff, open up. We know you're in there. Help me find my boy, damn you. What's a skakato?"

Inside, Rackem cowered in the corner of his room and poured whiskey down his throat. Rackem feared Skudakumooch. He could not bear to hear its name. He could not endure the shame of what he had done.

"Open up I say!" Talbert thumping on the door. "Get out here and help me!"

It did no good. Rackem was a drunk coward, sniveling with his box in the darkness.

"Maybe I can help you, Talbert," Larissa said. She was too kind, putting a hand on Talbert's shoulder to stop him from breaking down Rackem's door. "I saw everyone who left last night from my window. I know who stayed. If your boy is in town, we can find him. There are not many places he could be. Not anymore. There are only the

Roscals, the Henleys, Pastor Marble, the Ashberrys, and a few others left. I think Pearl and Dennis, Thomas Weathers and his parents. I'm not sure about a witch, but if one of the people in Emmert has your boy, it has to be one of them."

Talbert sighed and lowered his fist from Rackem's door. Probably best not to tell Miss. Huntly that he had killed Pearl Tanner, that she had killed her husband. Talbert didn't need Larissa running off scared. She appeared to be the only person able to help him. Perhaps together they could find whoever took his son. Maybe if they found the children and got out of town, whatever godless curse haunted Emmert would die. Perhaps if he got Lani to Fort Boise her mind would heal.

"Okay," Talbert said. "You and me, Miss. Huntly. We're going to find my boy and the other children before night swallows us whole."

3

Someone started screaming inside Mrs. Ashberry's house. Talbert and Larissa were in the road, about to mount their horses and set off when the sound reached them. "Johnathon?" Talbert said.

Again, someone screamed. Though it was more of a yelp, a young man's high-pitched squeal of pain.

"Johnathon!" Talbert was wild. It sounded like his boy was screaming in agony. And just across the street—just there in Mrs. Ashberry's house!

Talbert made a break for it. He sprinted through the dirt and onto Mrs. Ashberry's porch, took two strides forward and kicked her door wide open.

"Johnathon?" Talbert stood frantic in the threshold, Mrs. Ashberry's door swinging on bent hinges. The fat lady stood by her kitchen table, holding Thomas' arm flat against it. She had the kid bound and gagged.

"Talbert," Mrs. Ashberry said, jolly jowls jiggling, "have you come for the stew? It's not ready yet, I'm afraid."

Talbert could hardly comprehend what Mrs. Ashberry

was doing. Johnathon was not there, yet she had Thomas strapped to chair at the head of her kitchen table. There was a bloody cleaver in Mrs. Ashberry's right hand, Thomas' arm cleaved into sections like a stick of celery: fingertips, knuckles, half a palm, a wrist, a chunk of forearm, all laid out in culinary procession.

Miss. Huntly burst into the doorway behind Talbert. She took one look at Thomas' mutilation and screamed.

"Silence," Mrs. Ashberry snapped. "You're not the only chef in town, Larissa." And Mrs. Ashberry swung her cleaver and hacked off the final slab of Thomas' forearm, leaving the knotted elbow bone spitting blood onto the table. Thomas rocked, sputtered gibberish, then passed out.

Talbert sputtered too. He had no words. His strength of moments ago was erased in the face of such evil. Thomas was unconscious, gagged and bleeding to death, while across the table from him was Mrs. Ashberry's husband. Though Walter was more skeleton than man, bones picked clean of their meat as if ravaged by crows, empty eye sockets staring across the table at Thomas, lipless teeth clenched in a smile.

"What have you done?" Talbert asked. His voice quavered with fear.

"I'm preparing a stew," Mrs. Ashberry said, casually as if there were not two mutilated people sitting at her kitchen table. Her nonchalance reminded Talbert of Pearl Tanner, how normal she had sounded when describing her perverse surgery.

"I made a delectable slow-cooked bicep yesterday." Mrs. Ashberry motioned behind her, to the black pot and the huge bone rising out of it like a primal cudgel. "Melted right off the bone. It was delicious. Far better than Thomas' cockmeat. That was like eating a chicken neck, all wrinkly skin and too much blood." She sighed, her chubby face filled with nostalgia. "It had just been so long since I had a young hard cock in my mouth. I had to try it, although it did taste better before I chomped it off."

Mrs. Ashberry turned and fetched an empty pot from the counter, moved back to the table and swept all of Thomas' mangled pieces into it, being sure to collect the spilt blood with the blade of her hand.

"Larissa, my dear, your breasts are quite large. Very firm. Perky and perfectly round. I'll bet Yohan loved to play with them before he croaked, nuzzling his face into them and squeezing his cock between them, lathering your chest with spit, maybe some oil. I'd like to try, if you wouldn't mind. Not to fuck them, as I have no cock." She lifted her blood-speckled shift to show Larissa and Talbert her mound of curly black hair, pressed upon by a fold of fat. "See? No cock. I would merely like to use the fat from your breasts to make something yummy. I'm not sure what. They just look so delicious, so plump. Mine were like that once, but they are too darn massive. They sagged to my belly before I was twenty-two."

"She's just like the rest," Talbert said, totally aghast before Mrs. Ashberry's horror. "She's mad. Bonkers. She's lost every bit of sense that God gave her. She's possessed, tainted, bewitched." Talbert shoved Larissa out the door, back onto the porch. "Run," he said. "Get out of here before she tries to eat you. I'll hold her off."

"Not without you." Larissa fought against Talbert, trying to pull him off the steps with her.

Mrs. Ashberry frowned at them, struggling like idiots in the doorway. "It's going to be like that, is it? Come into my home, uninvited, interrupt my cooking, then leave without having the curtesy to try something? Unbelievable. I can see it from you, Larissa. You're a good for nothing whore and everyone knows it. But you, Talbert. You are politer than anyone in Emmert. For you to refuse my hospitality is an insult."

Mrs. Ashberry picked up her cleaver. "Come and

sit," she said, moving around the head of the table where Thomas was slouched forward, blood trickling out of his stump. He looked dead. "Talbert, sit and enjoy my stew. Miss. Huntly, give me the fat from your breasts. I'll cut them off nice and easy. You won't even know they're gone."

She was closing in on them. Talbert could see the hunger in Mrs. Ashberry eyes, the cleaver brandished as if to bury it in someone's head. She bellowed, "Let me taste you," and charged at them.

Talbert pushed Larissa out of the way just in time to take the full brunt of Mrs. Ashberry's assault. She tackled Talbert straight through the banister in an explosion of splinters. Talbert landed on his back and got the wind knocked out of him. Mrs. Ashberry crashed and rolled like a big, fleshy boulder in the street. She got up and started yelling. "You are rude. Give me your meat!"

She was quick for a fat lady. Talbert lay there wheezing and Mrs. Ashberry trampled him, her huge foot crushing Talbert's gut. She stampeded towards Larissa, too fast for the frightened woman to move. Mrs. Ashberry rammed into her, knocking Larissa onto her back. Then Mrs. Ashberry loomed above her, pudgy lips moist, cleaver poised to crack open Miss. Huntly's face. Mrs. Ashberry snarled. "You've always been a little—"

A shot rang out, deafening like a great crack of thunder. Mrs. Ashberry's brains burst out the back of her skull and she crumpled to the ground in a great heap of flesh.

4

Frank refused to get out of bed. It had been two days since the disaster at the Henley's farm and Frank was a sulky mess. A dozen brave men had gone to catch a predator and get Frank's daughter back, and instead one child was clawed to shreds like poor Edgar and two more children were stolen. Not to mention the exodus. The whole damn town picked up and left in wake of the supposed witch. Not that Frank blamed them. He would have gone too if not for Noel. But she was out there somewhere, held captive by whatever hell spawn tormented Emmert. Frank couldn't leave without his daughter. Though he was damned if he had any idea where to look for her. Frank was destitute, depressed and grief-stricken in bed.

"Sky's on fire," Betsy said. She stood in the doorway of their bedroom and frowned, Frank cowering beneath his blanket like a sick child.

"I ain't surprised," Frank said. "It's probably Hell rising, tearing down Heaven. The worlds gone to the dogs. Come and lay down, Bets, let's be incinerated together."

"Quit your blithering, Frank. Get out of bed and come look at this. The darned sky is on fire because it's setting. Reddest sunset I've ever seen. The whole darned sky is boiling. Not a speck of pink or orange or yellow. All red."

"That so?" Frank raised an eyebrow. "Didn't we just wake up?"

"We did just wake up, Frank. And now it's dusk. Looks like them folks was right. There's witchery afoot. Looks like the end of times out there."

Frank sighed and began to squirm out of bed. "Suppose I best see for myself. If the world really is ending, we ought to be together, Bets."

There was a knock on the door. Frank's eyes bulged and he stared at Betsy. "Who is it?"

Betsy frowned. "How should I know, Frank? You best get up and answer it. Could be Rackem. He could have news of Noel."

Frank leapt out of bed. "You really think so?" And ran to answer the door, scrawny in nothing but his cotton breeches.

But it was not Rackem knocking on the door. It was Pete Roscal. He stood grinning on their stoop, short and filthy and covered in a gross black sludge. It dripped from his ears and trickled off his bulbous nose, oozing from the corners of his mouth like black drool.

Frank stared at him. "The heck happened to you, Pete?"

"I went for a lovely dip in a bog," Pete said. "I liked the way the slime felt on my skin, so I brought it home with me." He tilted his head back and laughed, tar frothing from his mouth.

Betsy nudged in beside Frank. "Heck happened to you, Pete?" He looked disgusting, like a swamp dwarf.

"Says he went for a swim in a bog," Frank said.

Betsy scrunched up her face. "A swim in a bog? What the heck for?"

"Someone was playing tricks on me," Pete said. "They had Angela strung up in a tree and I had to climb to get her down. Bats had nested in her belly. I think one of them shit on me." Pete inspected himself, as if able to tell shit from whatever runny gunk seeped from his pours.

Frank and Betsy exchanged a worried look. Something was quite wrong with Pete. He was acting crazy, eyes two big saucers of blackness. Behind him, the sky raged and billows of red clouds rumbled with thunder.

"What of Noel?" Frank asked. "Did you find her?"

"Yeah," Betsy said. "Did you find her?"

"Noel is safe and sound," Pete said. "Safe as a bound hound in a man's pound." Again, he tilted his head and cackled hysterically.

"Say true?" Frank nearly grabbed Pete by his shirt—but Frank didn't want to touch the gross little man. "Where is she?"

Pete stopped tittering and focused his black eyes on Betsy. When he spoke, his voice was all chewed up. "Did you know you're pregnant? Six weeks, I'd reckon. Got a baby in your belly. It's so smelly, I'd eat it like jelly." Pete did a psychotic dance on the porch, rods of lightning striking the tops of trees and setting them ablaze. "Come,"

Pete said. "Come and I'll show you what I've done for fun. You can say hi to Noel. Yes, say hi to Noel before we all burn in Hell."

5

Rackem just about fell down the steps trying to holster his gun. He dropped it and the bulky thing clattered down the stairs and he grabbed hold of the railing to steady himself. Then he sat down hard and vomited between his legs.

Miss. Huntly trembled on the ground. "She tried to kill me... Mrs. Ashberry was going to kill me."

Talbert rushed to help Larissa up, his insides throbbing from where Mrs. Ashberry had stepped on him. "Mrs. Ashberry wasn't herself," he said, hoisting Miss. Huntly to her feet. "She was possessed by whatever evil has invaded Emmert. It's gotten into everybody. Pearl, Pete, Lani. It's turning our friends into savages. I'm not sure why it hasn't affected us."

"There is no reason," Rackem said, grunting as he bent to pick his pistol out of the dirt. "Skudakumooch spreads its corruption indiscriminately. The three of us got lucky. Had the rest of the town stayed, I'm sure half of them would be just as deranged as Mrs. Ashberry by now."

Larissa whirled and pointed a finger at Rackem. "You shot her!" She was hysteric. "You killed Mrs. Ashberry. And...and...Mrs. Ashberry killed her husband. My Lord, Rackem, she killed Thomas. That poor boy. She...she cut him into pieces and ate him."

Larissa spun in a circle, away from Talbert and collapsed onto her bum in the middle of the road. "I should have left with the others." Talking to herself now. "I'm still young. Lord knows I could have started a new life in the East. I could have remarried. I could have had children. Now look at me. I'm going die in this rotten town. Just look at the sky." She raised her hands, gesturing to the red storm and the rumbles of thunder. "Emmert is besieged by the forces of darkness. The people have gone mad. I'm doomed. Totally doomed."

Larissa got up in a huff, stormed over to Rackem's porch. "Give me one good reason not to walk out those gates right now." Larissa pointed at Emmert's open gates, the endless storm raging beyond them over the flatlands.

"Don't reckon you'd get very far," Rackem said. He spat in the dirt, jammed a crinkled cigarette in his teeth. "She's got us now. That's her storm that reddens the sky. I reckon you'd get eaten by wolves or struck by lightning. Besides, Talbert needs your help to find his boy."

"You know where he is?" Talbert moved beside Larissa. He stared down at Rackem, his mutilated ear bleeding once more from being tackled through Mrs. Ashberry's banister.

"No." Rackem shook his head. "But I think it's about time I told you a story, Talbert. Why don't you and Miss. Huntly take a seat. I'll tell you what plagues our town. I'll tell you about the witch who's taken your son."

Talbert glanced at Larissa. She mouthed, *skakatoo*, and folded her skirt to sit beneath Rackem in the road. Her and Talbert were already filthy. A little more dirt didn't matter. They sat like children with their legs crossed and listened to Rackem's story.

6

Larissa had already heard the first part, about Rackem's crummy childhood and his time with the Indians. The rest was new.

"She gave birth to my children," Rackem said. "Twins. A boy and a girl. We raised them happily enough. She learned to speak God's language and we lived together in solitude, a few goats and a couple chickens. We planted corn."

"In Emmert?" Talbert asked.

"No. Southwest of here. Do you want to talk or listen?"

Talbert shut up.

"The kids were two. I won't say their names. I can't bear to repeat them. It happened around this time of the year, when they were two, when the weather was warm and the sun shined late into the evenings. I never noticed anything wrong. How could I have? She started going off into the woods late at night. I thought it was an Indian thing. I said nothing. Then she quit speaking altogether. She wouldn't even look at me. She spent all her time staring at the children, especially when they slept. I thought maybe she missed her people."

Lightning illuminated the churning red sky and for a moment, Rackem looked like a corpse, his beard alabaster, his features rotten beneath the wide brim of his hat.

"I went to check on some snares at the edge of the wood. Two rabbits were caught and twitching in them, somehow still alive with their necks broken. I had to slit their throats to stop them fidgeting. When I got back to the cottage it was dark. Her and the kids were gone. I thought she had taken them back to her tribe. I was ready to ride upon them with all the fury of God. If only that had been the case.

"I followed a set of tracks by candlelight and found them in the northern forest, in a small clearing. The kids were scared. I remember their little faces, soft brown with my rugged features, strong and good looking. She stood behind them, a hand on either's shoulder. She watched the grove of trees in front of her. She was so focused. I had no idea what she was doing.

"I tried to take my children back. I was strong back then. I had power and muscles, for all the good they did me. I got too close and she picked me up by my throat and threw me against the trunk of a redwood tree. I thought my back was broken. I slumped against it and couldn't move.

"Then the ground started to shake. Leaves and

pinecones fell on my head. I heard the rustle of tall branches as something huge made its way towards the clearing. Then I saw it. Taller than three men, its skin gray and in the moonlight translucent, kind of decayed. Fire burned in its eyes, small embers within an inhuman mask. She, my Indian woman, bowed before this walking Nephilim and presented it with my children. It took them, one in each hand, screaming and crying for help.

"I was crippled. I couldn't get up. All I could do was watch as the beast ate them raw. It held my offspring by their long black hair and bit off chunks of their flesh. They shrieked in pain, wriggled and gushed blood onto the dark grass. Then they died, but not before enduring more agony than our lord and savior, Jesus Christ, ever had. The sinewy forest ghoul slurped my children's organs from wounds in their bellies and tossed them aside like trash. Then it ripped my Indian woman's head off. It grabbed her skull with one hand and yanked, pulled her spine out of her body and left her in a mess of gore. It stalked out of the clearing, everything I had ever loved mutilated and disfigured in the moonlight."

Larissa's mouth was agape. For once in her life, she had no words. Talbert rubbed his scruffy chin. It sounded insane to him, too unreal. How could God permit such a creature to exist?

"Is this true," Talbert asked. "Your wife and children were slaughtered by a monster?" Despite all that had happened, Talbert still found it hard to believe.

Rackem was staring at his hands. He had a look of sadness about him that Talbert had never seen before, not in anyone. "I had to bury them," Rackem said. "My children and my woman. I buried them in the woods where the monster had come from, the southern woods behind Talbert Schmidt's farm. I put their bones in a box and buried it under a tree. Then I went up the hill, walked a while through the prairie and collapsed. I built a small cottage for myself. I couldn't return to the old one. It's probably still there, decaying on the other side of the woods. After a while, people came. Emmert was born. I drowned the memory of my family with whiskey for twenty years."

"But then you dug them up," Larissa said, all the pieces coming into focus. "You did, didn't you? That's why the box is in your house. You went out there and dug up your wife's bones."

Rackem nodded. His head was hung in shame and he did not look at her.

"And when you dug your wife's bones out of the ground... What? The monster came back? I don't understand."

"Skudakumooch must have been dormant," Rackem said, "sleeping in the woods. When I opened the box to look once more upon my family's bones, the stain of its evil seeped into the world and called it forth. She must have come that night from the forest and taken Johnathon. Skudakumooch is an Indian witch who feasts on the flesh of children and corrupts the minds of townsfolk. Her evil has been gnawing on Emmert for nearly a week. It's a miracle any of us are still sane."

"Why didn't you say something?" Talbert asked. He got up and approached the sheriff, so angry he felt like slapping the hat of Rackem's head. "Why didn't you warn us?"

"I wasn't sure," Rackem said. "Not until I saw the shredded body of the Henley's daughter. Only then did I know without a doubt it was Skudakumooch. I had thought it a prowler who took your boy, maybe a psychotic vagabond camping out in the bush. I thought we could catch whoever it was. After so many years, I never believed the witch would return to plague our town."

"Looks like you were wrong," Talbert said. "Whether it be a witch or the Devil himself, something has come to Emmert. It's killed people, Rackem. It's plunged Lani's mind into chaos. It's taken my boy. And now you're telling me Johnathon's set to be eaten by a goddamned creature?" Talbert was mad. Thunder rolled across the fiery heavens and he yelled, "You're supposed to be the sheriff! Why are you hiding in your house, drunk on whiskey? Damnit, Rackem, we need to get my boy back."

"There may be time," Rackem said. "If Skudakumooch had devoured your son, she'd have left his remains. It's more likely she's corrupted someone in town, same as she did with Mrs. Ashberry. She must be using whoever it is to keep the children alive until she needs them. And now, with the rest of Emmert gone to Fort Boise, there are no more children for her to eat. I'm afraid when darkness falls, Skudakumooch will come for Johnathon and the others."

CHAPTER TEN

1

Talbert was mad. Him and Larissa were starting down the Emmert Road on horseback and Rackem was still at his house drinking whiskey. The sheriff claimed he had an important job to do, that he needed to ensure the future safety of all those who lived in Emmert. It felt like an excuse to Talbert. An excuse to get drunk and watch the world end.

"I can't believe he won't help," Talbert said. "Twelve years I've known Rackem. And now, in our final hour, he balks. It's disgraceful."

"I'm sure he has his reasons," Larissa said. "It sounded important, whatever Rackem must do. Our sheriff may drink too much, but he's still our sheriff. I believe he has Emmert's best interest in mind. He's doing what he thinks is right in the eyes of God."

Talbert grunted. He was mad nonetheless. He didn't care what Rackem was doing.

They were passing Logan Reitner's workshop and Carlos O' Brian's store. It was creepy in the red dusk, cold wind swirling through the street. Carlos' sign clattered in the wind and Logan's forge was dead. Seeing it like that made Talbert sad, thinking no more horseshoes would be forged by Logan's strong hands. It seemed to him like Emmert was already lost. God had condemned their town. So much for a bountiful life in the west.

They passed Mr. Beucanon's massive estate, the silo behind his house towering in the sky. It looked like a castle tower in the dying sunset, bricks washed red with the blood and fire of some nearby battlefield. Talbert felt inside his waistband for the pistol Rackem had given him. He didn't like the weight of it.

"Where are we going?" Larissa asked.

"The Oswalds didn't kidnap their own daughter," Talbert said. "Thomas Weathers was butchered and no one has seen Stanley or Lucile. Pastor Marble is too old to snatch a child, never mind keep one captive. Pearl and Dennis are dead. That leaves us with Pete Roscal."

"Pete?" Larissa's voice was a scream in Talbert's ear. "You really think Pete has the children?"

"Pete was in an awful huff when I saw him last," Talbert said, "cursing at the townsfolk. I'd not be surprised if it was Pete who unearthed little Angela's grave, God bless her soul. Might be he's got the kids trapped in his shed and doesn't even know it. The witch's evil seems to make people dumb to their crimes. I've known Mrs. Ashberry twelve years. She'd never have hurt young Thomas if not for the witch's infernal influence."

"Infernal influence indeed," Larissa said. She held tight to Talbert's waist as they trotted through a dying world of corruption. Everywhere Miss. Huntly looked were aspects of the witch's pollution. It had spread through Emmert like a disease. They went past Mrs. Henley's school where the orchard had wilted and rotten fruit sat decaying in the grass, where unshapely forms loitered in the dead grove like ghosts in a graveyard.

Then they were at Pastor Marble's church, transformed by the witch's heresy into a purgatory for the accursed. Shadows wandered forsaken through the grounds. Malformed specters danced on the roof and a bolt of lightning set the wooden cross ablaze, shadows prancing around the burning cross in defiance of God. Pastor Marble had hung himself from the rafters and swung beyond the doorway of the church, his face blue and bloated and more of the ugly ghosts swatting at him in a riotous crowd.

Everywhere they looked was ruin and sacrilege, natural things dead as if in the throes of winter and perverse apparitions rummaging through the property of those who had once been virtuous, picking at their waste and pillaging their homes. They skulked through yards, these shadows, these manifestations of the witch's sin. They lingered behind windows as spooky silhouettes. They regarded Talbert and Miss. Huntly with hideous black grins.

"Let's stop at the Weathers' place," Larissa said. "It's just there. No one has seen them in days. We should see if they're alright."

Talbert reluctantly agreed. He dismounted and walked through Lucile's dead flower garden and knocked on the door. No one answered. Talbert went around back. He hoisted himself up on the first windowsill he found and was looking into Stanley and Lucile's bedroom. In the waning daylight he could see them clearly. Stanley and Lucile were entwined on their bed, sex organs mashed together and their groins all red and blistered. Lucile had a belt lashed around her neck and her face was terribly swollen. In a dark corner of the room were two shadows hunkered with their backs to Talbert, jittering as they laughed.

He let himself down and went back to Larissa. "Let's go," Talbert said, mounting his horse. "Stanley and Lucile are dead."

The Henley's lane was pitch black when they passed it, no light at all emanating from their farmhouse. Talbert wondered how they were faring with two children gone and one murdered. He wondered how Clyde and Retha were dealing with Emmert's demise, with the rise of the witch's evil and the haunts spilling into their town.

Then Talbert's horse gave up. He had already been moving slowly, and as they neared the Roscal's farm the horse gave a grunt and kneeled to let Talbert and Larissa climb off. With one final breath of air, the horse died. Just died, rolled over and stopped breathing.

"God help us," Talbert said, crossing his heart.

2

Frank Oswald was waiting for them at the mouth of the Roscal's lane. Talbert mistook him for a shadow, another one of the witch's tricks. Frank stood in the burnt dusk like a despondent soldier, half cast in shadow and ragged in his flimsy breeches.

"Betsy's with child," Frank said. His head was hung, whole posture slack. Something about the way he stood made Talbert nervous.

"Congratulations," Talbert said. "All the more reason to get our kin back and leave town before it's too late."

"It's already too late," Frank said. "She's inside of me, in me head. I can feel... something." Frank looked up, his eyes two huge pupils weeping a black discharge down his cheeks. "It's in my soul, Talbert." Frank took a hard step forward. "It's got me sick." And puked a black, chunky slop into the dirt. "It's a thousand voices screeching in me head, calling for violence."

Talbert stepped away from Frank and put his hand on Rackem's pistol. Something was wrong. Skudakumooch had gotten to Frank, infiltrated the man's mind and made him volatile. There was a look of anger in his blackened eyes that frightened Talbert, a look of unfiltered violence. And here, blocking the path between Talbert and his son!

He took the pistol from his waistband and pointed it at Frank. Then Talbert cocked the hammer back, a ball of lead wrapped in cloth at the bottom of the barrel, ready to be fired. "Get out of our way, Frank. Nothing will keep me from my boy." Talbert's hand shook. He was so nervous.

Frank snarled. "It's too late, Schmidt. Darkness falls. Your boy is ours." He lumbered forward, ungainly like he couldn't control his body. Black sludge bubbled from his mouth.

Talbert screamed. "I'll not leave without my boy!" And pulled the trigger.

The bullet nearly missed. Larissa shrieked as Frank's throat was ripped apart, like a dog had bitten the side of his neck off. His life spritzed out of him in a mist of blood and Frank dropped to his knees. "It's too late," he wheezed, black blood frothing out his lips.

Then Frank fell sideways in the dirt, blood gushing from the tear in his throat. That was when darkness eclipsed Emmert. The sun had finally set.

3

Sheriff Rackem plodded down the steps of his home and into the street, nightfall saturating the world in darkness. He walked over the mound of flesh that had once been Mrs. Ashberry, flicking ash from his cigarette onto her as he went. He climbed the stairs and entered the dead woman's house.

Candles flickered on the kitchen table, yellow light dampening Thomas Weather's lifeless face. Rackem ruffled the kid's hair as he moved to the other side of the table and shoved Mr. Ashberry's decayed skeleton out of its seat. It rattled to the floor in a pile of snapped bones. Rackem sat in Walter's chair and propped his feet on the table, leaned back and grumbled to himself.

Walters skull sat atop a heap of femurs and ribs, tibias and fibulas. And it looked at Rackem with hollow, laughing sockets. Green strips of gangrenous flesh clung to Walter's forehead plate, nose starch white, yellow mandibles smiling.

"What the are you looking at?" Rackem flicked his cigarette into one of Walter's eye sockets. The ember fizzled and it looked like the skull was winking at him. "Don't judge me. It wasn't I who carved the flesh from your bones. I'm just here to clean up the mess."

Rackem rolled a cigarette and stood up, raised his

Witch Bones

boot high and brought it down on Walter's skull, shattering it to dust. Rackem picked up a candle from the table and used it light his smoke. Then he went about the room, to Mrs. Ashberry's front window. He caught a glimpse of his ugly reflection in the glass and groaned. "Wasted old drunk. Look at what you've done."

Sighing, Rackem held the candleflame to the curtain and set it alight. "I just wanted to talk to you again." He moved around the room, lighting more curtains on fire, then into the parlor and he placed the candle on Mrs. Ashberry's fabric rocking chair. "How was I to know she'd return?" He stood in the doorway, watching the rocking chair catch flame. "How was I to know there would be such ruin?"

Rackem left Mrs. Ashberry's house with smoke wafting out the doorway. The fire would spread. It was too hungry not to.

Down the street in Carlos O' Brian's general store, Rackem rummaged through the shelves for a canister of kerosene. He drenched the counter and floor in it. Before he left, Rackem tossed a match into the store and a carpet of flame spread throughout the place. Soon, it would travel in rivulets of orange and red and consume the entire building.

Rackem stood in the street and adjusted his wide brim hat, dusty in his coat. He watched billows of black smoke migrate through Logan Reitner's smashed windows, the etching of the Virgin Mary shattered into colorful shards in the grass. A hole opened in the roof and rubble crumbled into Logan's house, a great belch of fire breathing into the sky. Rackem was glad the townsfolk had run away. There was no one to witness the death of Emmert.

3

Their nervous eyes blinked in the darkness, whimpering and afraid. They reeled from the oafish hand that pawed at them through the bars, their tormentor cackling sickly as he prodded them like animals. He opened their cages one by one and yanked them out, unable to flail or scream because the children were shackled and muted. Pete pulled them from the cages in the back of his shed and attached leashes to their collars. Then he dragged them across his lawn. The kids were starved, malnourished, thirsty. They stumbled on all fours like a pack of abused dogs pulled onwards by their cruel master. Pete never stopped laughing.

"Mush, you mongrels!" Yanking on their leashes, guiding the children towards the great pyre Pete had erected in his yard. The fire cast a ring of orange light around itself, some unholy halo. "Mush, mush!" Pete booted the children one by one as he wrangled them into the circle of light. "Filthy animals."

Their faces were ghoulish and emaciated in the firelight. Some of them knew death was imminent, though none of the children comprehended exactly what death meant. They were just kids. They were scared and eager to be out of the shed, even if it meant the end for them. Their time in there had been hell. The cold night air was a kiss from God on their skin compared to the stagnant, piss-filled air of Pete's shed, where they had been forced to shit and piss in their cages and roll in their feces as they slept. Pete had crammed crow feathers down their throats to make them vomit. It was the only food he had given them, diseased crow meat that had made them sick. Last night, Pete had pinched each child's tongue to their bottom lip with a pair of tongs, then sewed them together with metal wire. All they could do was garble sounds of pain.

Pete lined them side by side in front of his bonfire, close enough that the heat scalded their skinny, underfed bodies. Then he stood before them and smiled at his abuse, at the primitive distention of the children's lower mandibles, the swollen redness of their mouths, the infected scabs where metal infused tongue and lip. "Filthy swine," Pete said.

He secured each child's dog collar to a stake he had

jammed in the ground behind their backs, keeping them rigid as slaves up for auction. Then Pete Roscal moved apishly about his four captured children, his stout body swaying with uncouth barbarity as he prodded the youngsters and barked at them. He knelt before Johnathon Schmidt and smiled his mucky smile, jabbed the boy hard enough in the eyes that Johnathon spewed bile onto Pete's face. Pete laughed and licked Johnathon's tears.

Noel Oswald whimpered, terrified as Pete hobbled like a dripping, bow-legged swamp monster to her and began to kick Noel savagely in the ribs. Noel grunted and squeezed her eyes shut, white stars exploding each time Pete kicked her in the gut.

The Henley's children he spat on. Pete cursed at Joel and Nancy in demonic tongues and spat globs of yellow-black slime onto their faces. "Filth," he said, and moved on, waddling strangely into the blackness beyond the firelight.

Moments later, Pete returned from the darkness dragging Betsy Oswald by her hair. She screeched and wriggled, naked and wrapped tightly in a long tendril of rope. She couldn't move her limbs. But she could scream.

"Noel," Betsy said, seeing her mutilated daughter propped near the fire. "Noel, my child. I love you." Then Betsy saw Pete's inferno, the steel shaft in its core. She saw her damnation and her heart sank. "Look away," Betsy said to her daughter. "Don't watch. It'll be over soon, my child. We will be in God's hous—"

Pete clubbed her in the face. "Don't say his name. He's abandoned you. His light is dead."

Noel cried for her mother as Pete hoisted Betsy into the flames and manacled her to the metal rod. The children all cried as they watched Betsy scream, her face melt like butter, the baby inside her belly roast as if in an oven.

4

"Pass me the bag," Talbert said, hurrying up the Roscal's lane in the darkest night imaginable. They could hear Betsy screaming, see the plume of red smoke wafting over Pete's house.

"Here." Miss. Huntly passed Talbert the small satchel of gunpowder so he could reload Rackem's pistol.

Talbert kept moving, turned the gun over in his hands and squinted to see the barrel, where he had to dump the gunpowder. Talbert had never used a pistol before. He hated the violence of such a thing. Yet Talbert had already killed two people. He'd kill a hundred more to get back his son.

He poured a bit of powder into the barrel and then jammed in a lead ball wrapped in cloth, still walking briskly up the lane. When Talbert tried to pass the gunpowder back to Larissa, it slipped between his fingers and sprinkled into the dirt.

"Oh no," he said. But it was too late. The powder was gone. Betsy's screams were echoing through the night like the cries of a banshee. They had to keep moving.

"You still have one shot, right?" Larissa asked. She was even more nervous than Talbert, the friendly widow thrown so suddenly into a night of brutality and violence.

"Yes." Talbert held the pistol against his shoulder, coming upon the Roscal's farmhouse now. "If I miss, I'll beat the scoundrel with my bare hands."

Betsy had stopped screaming, but the pain of her wails somehow lingered in the air. Talbert sprinted around the Roscal's house with Larissa by his side, the light from Pete's fire flickering in the grass. Then they were around it, dashing across Pete's lawn while the madman danced about his fire, Betsy's corpse charred in the flames like an overcooked scarecrow.

"Dear God in Heaven," Talbert said, gasping as they neared the ring of light and he saw the four children tied to their posts. "Johnathon, is that you? Johnathon?" He recognized the boy's scruffy brown hair, combed so many times by Talbert's own fingers. Yet Johnathon didn't move. He was stuck. Pete had him chained up like a dog. "I'll kill you," Talbert roared, and made a mad dash for Pete with Rackem's gun drawn.

"Talbert," Pete said. He was prancing about the fire, face all sooty, evil grin too big for his mouth. "How good of you to come. She's on her way, I say, stomping through the forest to fuck up your day." Pete tilted his head back and cackled. All Talbert could smell was Betsy Oswald's roasting flesh.

Talbert stopped. He was at his wit's end, sick of the lunatics running free in his town, murdering and torturing and smiling at Talbert like everything was fine, like how Pete smiled at him now while Betsy's flaming husk began to disintegrate in the fire. It was godless. All of it. The Indian witch, the possessions—all of it without God. Children had been killed. Innocents had been corrupted. And now Talbert's boy was tied to a stake while Rackem's fairytale monster marched through the night to suck out his organs. To hell with that. To hell with Pete's mad cackling. Enough was enough.

Talbert lifted Rackem's pistol. He took four great strides and pulled the trigger and blew a fucking hole in Pete's chest.

Pete didn't make a sound. Chunks of lung exploded out his back in a mess of gore and sizzled in the fire. Pete staggered, tripped on some coals and fell into the flames. His body boiled and bubbled like burning pitch.

Talbert dropped the pistol and ran to his son. "God almighty," he said, kneeling to look upon Johnathon's mutilated face, "what's that bastard done to you?"

Johnathon tried to speak, but his tongue was stitched to his lip and he could only grunt.

"No." Talbert ran his finger gently along the sutures in Johnathon's lip. "Don't speak. You're alive.

That's all that matters. I love you so much and your alive."
Talbert was crying tears of joy, tears of sadness. He
struggled to get Johnathon's collar off. "We'll get you help.
There's a good doctor in Fort Boise. Mr. Ringall is there.
We can undo all this madness. We can start again."

Johnathon's collar came undone and he collapsed
into Talbert's arms. Finally, after wading through a shallow
hell, Talbert had reclaimed his boy. Johnathon was alive,
breathing and his face pressed into Talbert's chest, father
and son weeping together softly. It felt like a lifetime ago
that Talbert had woke to find Johnathon missing. Every
second since then had been madness.

"Praise God," Talbert said. "Praise God it's over.
Praise God you're alright, my boy. I'll never let anyone
hurt you again."

Miss. Huntly went around and unshackled the rest
of the children, all traumatized and in desperate need of
medical attention. Noel kept glancing into the fire, a look
of utter desolation on her young, mangled face. Her
mother's body had turned to ash.

"Look at what he's done," Larissa said. "What
kind of monster does this to children? Who, Talbert?
Who does this?"

Talbert rose, unable to take his hand off
Johnathon. He needed to feel his child, even if it meant
keeping one finger on his shoulder. "It's over now," he
said. "Pete's dead. We must get the children out of
Emmert while there's still time."

"You don't think..."

"I don't know." Talbert was looking beyond Pete's
fire, into the hollow night. "If the witch is out there, she
might still come for them. I need you to take the children
through Emmert's gate and start down the road towards
Fort Boise. I'm going to get Lani. Johnathon's safe with
you. It's all that matters now." Talbert smiled and touched
his son's chin, all the sadness of the world bubbling in little
Johnathon Schmidt's eyes. "I can't leave my wife here to

die."

5

Talbert hoped that with Johnathon safe and sound, the Indian witch's spell over Lani would be broken. He had expected to find her on the front porch waiting for him. But she wasn't there. Talbert bumbled through the darkness of their home, shouting, "Lani? Lani, where are you?"

Not in the house. Talbert ran out back. The emptiness had no end and he screamed into the eternal night, "Lani? Lani, where are you?"

Talbert ran through his pasture, searching madly for Lani as he screamed her name. "Lani, my love, where are you? I've found Johnathon. It's time for us to go." It was not until he crested the hill behind his house and looked down at the southern forest that he saw something, a humanoid shape moving in front of the tree line, the wall of creepy timbers where the forest began. It looked enough like Lani, kind of spectral. Talbert thought it was her nightgown glowing white in the darkness.

He went to her, floundering down the hill like a madman. Yet just as Talbert neared the barricade of trees, she glided into them, vanishing ghostly into the forest's even blacker darkness.

"No!" Talbert reached as if he could catch her. "Lani, come back. Don't go in there."

He came to a stop before the great and ominous wood. "Lani..." Talbert's voice soft, forlorn. "Lani, please..." He could not bear the thought of his beloved wife wandering insane through the forest. He had rescued Johnathon. Talbert would be damned if he would leave his wife to rot in the woods.

"I'm coming," Talbert said. He stepped through the trees, swallowed by the murk of the forest.

6

The whole town had been set ablaze. Larissa stood at the

southern gate with the four children, the sky on fire and the view through the open gateway like the view through the gates of Hell, one massive inferno.

Rackem emerged from the smoke, menacing in his duster and wide brim hat like the Devil come to collect new souls. He had a cigarette in his mouth, a dour expression on his face and a can of kerosene in one hand. His eyes brightened when he saw the children with Miss. Huntly.

"You found them." Rackem almost smiled. He was covered in soot and ash.

"What in the name of Christ is going on, sheriff?" Larissa asked. She stood protectively in front of the kids. "The whole town burns."

"It must. So long as the witch lives, none who farm this land will be safe. I must burn Emmert to the ground." Then Rackem touched her shoulder, noticing the way she guarded the youngsters. "You'd have made a good mother, Larissa. You might yet. The way is not so treacherous. Stick to the road and away from the fires. Leave Emmert while the light still holds back the dark."

"What's that supposed to mean?" Miss. Huntly jabbed Rackem in the chest with her finger. "What have you done? I demand an explanation. Where am I supposed to go? What am I supposed to do with these kids?"

Rackem merely sighed, stepped around her and looked down at little Johnathon Schmidt in his tattered bedclothes, the cruel metal sewed through his lip and tongue. It was nice to see the boy's face, even if he was disfigured. "Where's Talbert?"

"Gone to fetch Lani."

"I see." Rackem frowned. He liked Talbert. He was a good man, a godly man. It was a shame Lani had been compelled to insanity by Skudakumooch, the same as Rackem's Indian woman had been. At least Talbert's boy would survive.

"The children are yours now," Rackem told Larissa. "Take care they make it to Fort Boise. You've done good. God's proud."

"Will you not come with us?" Miss. Huntly was overwhelmed and afraid. She wanted Rackem's help. The way ahead was made of fire and behind them lay the darkness of the witch's long night.

But the sheriff shook his head and walked off. "Good luck, Miss. Huntly." And the spurs of his boots jingled as he strolled down the road.

She wanted to chase after him, to bang on Rackem's chest and demand he help her. But Larissa could not. She had the kids. She had Talbert Schmidt's boy and had promised to keep him safe. "Goodbye, sheriff," she muttered. And she corralled the children in front of her. "Let's go. It's time to leave."

7

The walk was long and hot. On both sides of the road houses crumbled into mounds of cinder. Emmert was destroyed, burning to ruin. Larissa led the children all the way to the front gate and beyond. Upon crossing the border, Larissa was left breathless by the serenity of the outside world. The sky was full of stars. Larissa hadn't seen the stars in days. Somewhere a wolf howled, a great white moon illuminating the west in a mellow, midnight glow. Everything just felt... normal. The chaos of Emmert was behind them.

Her and the children walked slowly through the night. Larissa smiled when she saw the sun rise in the east. She thought of Talbert. She thought of all Emmert's lost souls.

J. Cortex

The End

Made in the USA
Middletown, DE
17 May 2021